GW00864973

"It is compel... ...olds the reader in thrall."
Books for Keeps

"*After the Darkness* is Michael Smith's first novel and heralds the arrival of a promising newcomer to this tricky genre of books for young adults."
Junior Bookshelf

"The real triumph of this novel is that it illustrates the plight of Jews in the Second World War in an almost unbearably human and memorable way."
Books for Keeps

"It is a powerful account of the suffering endured by one Jewish family as they make a desperate dash for freedom . . . Strongly recommended."
Carousel

Boston!
Boston!

Michael Smith

POOLBEG

Published 1997 by
Poolbeg Press Ltd,
123 Baldoyle Industrial Estate,
Dublin 13, Ireland

© Michael Smith 1997

The moral right of the author has been asserted.

The Publishers gratefully acknowledge the support of The Arts Council.

A catalogue record for this book is available from the British Library.

ISBN 1 85371 885 8

Cover illustration by Tom Roche
Cover design by Poolbeg Group Services Ltd
Set by Poolbeg Group Services Ltd in Goudy 11.5/14.5
Printed and bound in Great Britain by
Cox & Wyman Ltd, Reading, Berks.

For Natasha, Susanna and Kate,
who are all here

Prologue

The Great Famine

In 1845, against the wishes of most of its people, Ireland was an integral part of Britain. Its population was estimated to have been more than 9 million, the vast majority of whom were so poor that they relied solely on the potato for food.

In 1845, 1846 and 1848 the potato crop in Ireland failed almost completely. Much of the other food grown in the country in those years was shipped to England, while small amounts of Indian corn, a cheap substitute for the potato, unfamiliar and unpalatable even to the starving, was sent to Ireland in a futile attempt by the government in London to alleviate the widespread distress.

Between 1845 and 1851 more than one and a half million Irish people died as a result of starvation or related illnesses. Two million or more emigrated, the majority to the cities of North America or Britain. Those who went as well as those who remained endured horrific privations.

During these years Ireland was in despair. Many of the landlords, unable or unwilling to collect rents from their tenants, were ruined. Others survived with their estates intact, and in the larger towns some of the merchants prospered. But for the poor the effects were unimaginable. Then, and for generations afterwards, the only hope was emigration. The wounds inflicted by the Great Famine were too deep to be forgotten. Wherever the emigrants went the scars remain.

Boston! Boston!

In January 1848 the Harbour authorities in Boston, Massachusetts received a report from a Swedish sailor who had been keeping night-watch on a ship lying at anchor off Battery wharf.

The man told of seeing a young woman – he was able to give only a scant description of her, she appeared to be hardly more than a child and was dressed in the poorest clothes imaginable – who had stood for almost an hour at the end of a cold windswept pier clutching a bundle to her chest. After some time the sailor had realised that the bundle contained a baby which the young woman rocked to and fro in her arms. Every now and then the feeble cries of the infant would carry across to the ears of the sailor, and the mother (for surely, the sailor said, it must have been the mother) would attempt to soothe it with soft words or a touch of her hand on its face. Eventually the wailing stopped, but the young woman made no attempt to leave the scene. She remained motionless at the edge of the wharf.

The sea at the foot of the wooden beams which supported the pier was reported to be near freezing that night. The water had heaved uneasily, the sailor said, too near frozen to slop or splash. It had glistened like oil, he told his listeners, as it gelled in the numbing air.

Then, he said, he had been distracted by the movement of another vessel nearby. He had looked away and almost immediately heard the sound of something hitting the sea's surface, but when he turned back to scan the water he could see nothing, neither the young woman nor the baby. He did not know how to swim, he confessed, so he had shouted for someone to go to their aid. But it was dark and the night was cold. No one had responded to his call. He had had to row ashore to get help and he had been too late to be of use.

The following morning the body of a newborn baby, not more than ten or twelve days old and wrapped only in rags, was found floating under the stern of a coastal schooner. The child was dead. There was no trace of the mother.

Chapter One

It was the first time Kate had ever been in the sea and she ventured in just far enough for the water to cover her ankles. She had been wandering on the beach for some time and particles of white shell and coral, crushed so fine it was like sand, still clung to her feet and glistened like stars on her dirty toes.

She held her long skirts up with one hand and with the other she blocked out the sun which, low in the late evening, fired the waves of the bay's surface so that it resembled a field of burning grass.

In a few seconds the lapping water had spread mounds of the ground coral all round her feet so that she seemed to be sinking slowly into the soft bed of the sea, but she was comforted by the feeling that her grip on the sand was becoming stronger and stronger with each wave which rippled past her.

Behind her, on the dunes which rose from the

beach, Tom and Liam lolled, leaning back on their elbows as they laughed together, hurling scallop and cockleshells into the air, making them spin and rise against the salt-sharp breeze drifting in from the Atlantic.

It was high summer and the July night was going to be long in coming. The water was warm, but Kate did not want to swim and she was content to cool her feet and immerse herself in this strange new world.

They had walked most of the day and the day before, all the way from Lough Inagh, where they lived, thirty miles away, to see the sea, to spend some time on the coast.

"With your aunt!" Kate's father had insisted as they set off.

"Under a hedge," Liam had whispered. "To hell with the aunt."

Kate turned to face the beach and the wind caught her dark blonde hair, dragging it around her shoulders and swinging it into her eyes so she had to close them. When she had cleared it from her face she noticed a pair of rabbits nibbling at the crown of one of the lower dunes where coarse grass grew in the season. The busy creatures grazed oblivious of the human life nearby, twitching their noses and mouths occasionally, but fearless, and plump from their efforts.

Liam O'Malley pushed himself up from the

ground and walked to Kate's side. He was two years older than his sister, almost a man. His sixteenth birthday had been only a week before and already he was as tall as his father with the hard brown hands and forearms of someone accustomed to a man's work. The cheekbones of his face were broad and prominent so that his eyes slanted away from his nose like a pair of blue almonds. Huge tan freckles lay everywhere on his skin as if fine autumn leaves had fallen on him, and the corners of his mouth turned up in a permanent grin. Indeed, he was a happy fellow. Kate could never be gloomy in his company. Of all her four brothers it was Liam she loved most.

"Tom and I are going to swim," he announced. "We're suffocated from the heat."

"Well, go on then. I'm not in your way." Kate often thought she liked Liam the most because she looked so like him. There were five other children at home, some older and some younger, but it was always Liam she felt part of, always Liam she wanted to be with.

She looked away and turned slowly back to face the line of rounded waves streaming into the bay. At first she had found herself almost afraid of the sea, of its ceaseless movement and its power which seemed to come from nowhere, and she had clutched Liam's hand for reassurance. She loved her brother too much to ever disagree with anything he said, but she was too happy at this moment to want to move away from him. She was happy to be on the beach, to have her feet cooled by the water, to have the sun on her face and the wind in her eyes. She was happy to know that the afternoon had not yet ended, that the weather looked as if it would hold for another day or two at least, that the laden fruit trees they had seen not far away would provide their supper.

Kate was happy too to be near Tom Lynch. But that last happiness she kept hidden. It was her only secret, the only thing she had not shared with Liam.

"Well, go on," she ordered. "Swim if you're going to swim."

Liam patted the clothes he wore, then held out his hands in a pleading gesture, begging her to go.

"I've seen your scrawny body before, Liam O'Malley. And I'll see it again I'm sure, a few times. So if you want to take off your clothes and swim, do so. I'm busy enough looking at the sunset."

"Tom wants to swim too," her brother muttered. "Couldn't you just go up the strand a bit? The dunes are here you see." He gestured at the only shelter on the beach. "No one looking from the road can see us here."

"You're my brother and Tom's your best friend.

8

I've known the pair of you since I was born. I don't know why you're fussing." But she smiled, and taking a step or two towards dry land, lowered her skirts to her wet ankles and kissed her brother on the chin.

As her lips touched Liam's face she saw Tom leap to his feet, but she would not allow herself to look in his direction. She began to move away, seeing a row of boulders some way along the beach and setting them as her destination.

Whoops of delight broke out from the two young men as soon as she turned her back to them. She heard them grunting with the effort of pulling off their clothes then, a few seconds later, came the sound of feet running on the hard sand and the slapping and splashing of water as they forced their way out through the waves.

Chapter Two

There was still plenty of heat from the low sun as Kate walked away, and she found herself enjoying the sensation of the sharp-edged sand scratching the hard soles of her feet. She swung her arms in an exaggerated manner so that her hands came up almost to her shoulders with each step she took and she began twisting her feet as she walked, so that the dry sand slid between her toes and squeezed out over the tops of her feet. The wind seemed to freshen as she drew further away from the dunes and soon she found herself bending into a stiff breeze which whipped her long, thick hair up and away from her face.

She could still hear the young men's shouts and the occasional thud which seemed to run along the surface of the beach as if they were jumping or falling on the sand, but she did not look behind her.

The strand narrowed where the boulders lay and there were no more dunes, just a series of long, low banks of sand dividing the sea from the scrubby grazing land which climbed away to the east, where the hills rose leisurely from the streams and turf bogs and a scatter of mean, mud cottages and rocky outcrops speckled the heat-deadened landscape.

In the distance nothing moved, but all around her there was life. A small furry form fled from her in a series of fluid leaps, bounding over stones and pieces of driftwood until it was out of sight. To her left, not far from the shore, three or four seals submerged themselves carefully at her approach, although Kate could only guess at what they were, as she had not seen a seal before. Shoals of fish appeared from time to time, leaping from the sea briefly as if they were birds, and shimmering in the silver sunlight. Crabs sidled away menacingly under rocks or into the greater safety of the sea while other, smaller things retreated sinuously, leaving only the trails of their bodies on the wet sand.

The seals attracted her interest most. When she came to the first of the boulders she stopped and leant back on the warm stone, tucking her hair out of the way into her shawl as she waited for the strange creatures to reappear. She could hear the insects and beetles of the beach moving at her feet but she kept her gaze only on the water. To her right the sun seemed bigger than ever as it neared the horizon, edging the waves with gold as one by one the seals' inquisitive heads reappeared, nosing the salt air cautiously and peering from side to side like sleek-coated dogs as they rose and fell with the swell of the water.

She knew they could see her but she remained motionless and in time they seemed not to mind her presence. After a while she realised they were two couples. One pair had moved away to float where she could hardly see them, in line with the sun's reflection on the water, until only two indistinct halos remained visible as their heads were eclipsed by the dazzling light of the sun.

The other pair were closer, no more than twenty or thirty paces from the shore and to her east so that she could see them more clearly. They began to roll about, close to each other, exposing more and more of their bodies and sending ripples far from their playground. Soon they were moving in unison, appearing almost to cling to each other, Kate thought, and thrusting their heads back and forth like the mating swans which spent their summers on the clear water of Lough Inagh where the O'Malley's cottage stood, not far from the Lynch's even smaller home.

Kate moved, intending to find a place to sit, but her sudden action disturbed the small animal she had seen earlier. It reappeared no more than two strides from her, a stoat, brown-backed and angry, rearing away from her, throwing itself up on to its hind legs to expose its white neck and belly. Its wide mouth yawned open and the two rows of sharp teeth gleamed as it seemed to draw breath. Then it shrieked wildly, a sound Kate had never heard before, a sound of such ferocity from an animal no bigger than a kitten that she cowered, flattening herself into the boulder behind her, her eyes never letting the creature from her sight. She found a high place to sit and, drawing her feet up as close as possible to her body and as far above the sand as she could, she screamed back at her challenger.

She feigned an attack, but the animal did not move and, regaining her composure, Kate saw the pale, fresh bones of another wild creature, a rabbit, she guessed. It had been killed a day earlier, and now lay between her and her enemy. She slipped from her perch, realising that the stoat was feeding its young or hunting, and that she would have to retreat. She made her way swiftly across the remaining boulders, away from the tiny predator and further away from the two young men who now, more than anything, she wanted to be near.

For a few yards the stoat followed her, letting loose with its piercing screams to hurry her on, and every now and then darting forward quickly and rearing at her as if in preparation for an attack. But its threats came to nothing and soon Kate reached the last of the boulders and ran across the beach to the grassy bank which, further along, formed the sheltering dunes where her brother had been. She kept to the highest ground, looking behind her nervously from time to time for the stoat, but it seemed to have forgotten her and she slowed her pace, allowing the lowering breeze and the warmth of the sun to ease her fright.

From her path she could see the dark heads of Liam and Tom as they swam, floating in the deeper water of the bay, and further on where the dunes rose she could look down on to the white gold of the strand and the serried waves, so low they were almost invisible, which queued to extinguish themselves on it.

When she came to the point on the dunes which lay immediately above the two swimmers she stopped and sat on a patch of wiry long-stemmed grass. She tucked her knees beneath her chin and drew her skirts over them until only her bare toes peeped out from below the rough cloth. She clasped both hands around her legs and gazed across the bay to where the heads of the young men were visible in the water.

On the knoll next to hers the two rabbits still munched steadily, but the seals could no longer be seen and the stoat too had vanished. Behind her a corncrake lifted its head and rasped its cry, while in the distance a donkey brayed, the sound rising and falling as the breeze carried it across to the beach. Suddenly Kate sensed a scuffle off to her left and then a cry could be heard, short and sharp and feeble. Where only a moment ago two rabbits had been feeding there was now only one to be seen, and that disappearing as fast as it could go, its white tail bouncing down the landward side of the dune towards the dry shelter of its warren.

Kate's eyes followed the frightened creature until it disappeared into a dark hole. Then she looked around for its companion.

A few moments later the rippling body of the predator flickered into view, dragging across the sand the limp body of the other young rabbit, resting from time to time and allowing its weight to fall to the ground, but never for a second relaxing the grip of its sharp, cruel teeth on the throat of its prey.

As soon as it could, the stoat made for the hard sand of the lowest part of the beach and there, where the going was easier, it picked up speed and soon disappeared against the sun's glare.

Chapter Three

Kate looked back to the two swimmers making their way slowly towards the beach. Their clothes lay in untidy heaps at the base of the dune and two trails of footprints led to the water's edge.

They were still playing, Liam fountaining water from both his hands and Tom plunging his clasped palms down below the surface to make the sound of a deep, distant drum, and all the time they were laughing and talking, calling to each other as if there was not another soul in their world.

Kate sat motionless as they approached the beach. Liam was the first to stand and she waited without interest as he used his hands to wipe the water from his arms and chest and legs. He called to his friend, but she could not hear his words. When Tom stood she found her mouth was dry and her breath seemed to catch in her throat. For a few seconds she stared at his body then, flattening herself to the ground, she slipped away over the back of the dune and out of sight.

By the time she made her appearance they were dressed. Liam ran to her as soon as he saw her and picked her up at the waist, spinning around with her in his arms and kissing her cheek and laughing.

Tom stood back, watching the brother and sister cavorting together as he brushed sand from his clothes. Finally, when Liam put his sister down, Tom spoke casually, his arms at his side, making no effort to approach his two friends.

"Can I have a turn at that?" he said, as if it was the most ordinary request in the world. His face was creased in a smile.

"Who are you asking?" Liam replied, looking from one to the other, but not as if he was at all surprised at his friend's question.

"I'm asking Kate," Tom said, looking at Liam. "You didn't think I wanted to swing you around and kiss you, did you?" They laughed again and when they stopped they were both looking at her.

At first she could not speak. She longed for Tom's hands to hold hers, and for his arms to be around her and holding her to his chest and face, but when her voice finally emerged from her mouth it was not her mind which spoke. "Please, no, Tom," she said firmly. "For God's sake." She found herself unable to look at his eyes and she stared at his tensed brown hands, listening all around her as if she suspected someone else might be speaking for her. "Where are your manners?" she asked.

Often, months later, during the days when she tried to forget that she had ever known Tom, when she wanted to wipe him forever from her mind, she still found herself surprised that such clean, firm-fingered hands could be capable of anything other than work, or perhaps a lover's touch.

"All washed away I suppose," Liam grinned, and he and Tom laughed again. Eventually Kate joined in and all three guffawed as if nothing at all had happened, as if Tom's request for a kiss had been something else, something of no importance, a suggestion that they walk along the beach perhaps, or throw stones into the water or lie beneath the shade of a tall tree and share each other's imaginings.

They sat in a silent line on the sand, Kate between the two boys, so utterly content to be with them that she thought her chest would burst with joy. None of the three felt a need to speak. They gazed out at the water as it flattened with the dying breeze. Nothing moved except for two of the seals which had moved further into the bay and suspended themselves inquisitively in the water opposite the motionless figures on the beach.

"We're not going to spend the night at Roundstone are we?" Kate asked. "I've walked enough for today. And the uncle and aunt, they'll hardly miss us will they?" Kate's aunt had married a fisherman, a dour older man whom they had met only once or twice. They had no wish to renew his acquaintance, especially not when they had each other and Tom for company.

"The hedge'll do fine," Liam told her, and he leaned over so that the top of his head lay against her neck.

"I'm for the hedge too," Tom agreed, and for a moment Kate held her breath, hoping that he too would lean over so she could feel the weight of his head on her shoulder. But only his hand touched her, brushing the side of her knee as he changed position on the sand.

For a long time no one spoke again and, as the day came to a close, Kate felt a fear creep up on her, as if something was about to be lost, some precious quality in the air which had made the day like no other. She had hardly a notion what it was which made this place, this sand, this bay, something she would live to remember, somewhere she had been unforgettably happy, completely at peace with herself. She felt tears welling in her eyes, but she held them back and it was not until Liam turned to look at her that she realised they were tears of joy. Then a smile of pure delight smothered her doubts and she cried and giggled at the same time, until her brother laughed with pleasure at the sight of her.

Chapter Four

Tom was the first to stand. "Dear God," he said, in awe of the sunset sky. "Where are we to be seeing a sight like that? The three of us, here!" His face was turned to the golden evening light. The face of a god, Kate thought, and his body tall and straight. A mass of black curly hair still damp from the sea was swept back from his forehead and his eyes were the colour of hazel cobs. "Where are we anyway?" he asked. "What is this place called?"

"Ballyconneely," Liam told him. "Back there on the road they said it was called Ballyconneely."

"Let's find the plum tree." Kate tipped her head up at Tom as Liam too got to his feet. He held out a hand to help his sister, but Tom was too quick for him and it was his salty grip which she felt, and his powerful pull which lifted her up. His eyes never left hers as her face rose towards him and, if she had not held herself back, their lips might have met. But she restrained her momentum, and when she was standing they simply smiled warmly as good friends do, although he kept hold of her hand for longer than was necessary.

Their shabby boots lay scattered at the end of the strand, but their feet, swollen from the day's walking and still warm from the sand, would not fit into them easily. They picked their way barefoot across the patch of rocky ground which separated the beach from the road and when they reached the rough, dusty track they turned north in the direction of Ballinaboy and Clifden.

The cloudless evening sky was the colour of heaven, Kate thought. Starlings wheeled above them in aimless, circling waves while black crows, more certain of their destination, flapped towards the wooded valleys where streams fed the stunted oaks and firs and rhododendrons and fuchsias which lined their banks.

It was not easy walking without shoes, although their feet were hardened enough by barefooted work in the fields of their fathers' tiny farms, and when they came at last to a stream which bubbled alongside the track they slipped down the bank and dangled their legs in the cool, black water until their swollen toes shrivelled and the smooth, peat-softened skin of their feet could be pushed without difficulty into their boots.

The coastline around them was formed of a series of deep inlets, heavily wooded in places, where the sea penetrated the land and washed away the vegetation from the rocks which lined it. Here, with the tide dragged west to America, mussels and limpets clung to the rocks, browned by the long, heavy strands of seaweed which hung in great festoons from every place in which a roothold could be found.

Small houses were spread haphazard across the land, most of them misshapen cottages of mud, without windows or doors and with smoke holes gaping in their roofs. A few, those of the stronger farmers, were more substantial, with two or even three rooms and windows, a proper chimney at one end, and gardens in which cabbages and flowers could still be seen in the twilight. All around, wherever there was open land, were fields of potatoes, neat rows of them, their foliage so dark it was almost black, lightened only by the small white flowers which adorned them in the height of July.

With nightfall the wind had dropped away to nothing and, by the time the three young people reached their destination, not a sound could be heard save for a few distant voices raised in song or argument.

The white-painted farmhouse they sought had two stories. On either side of the door was a pair of tiny windows, above and below. A thicket of firs protected the house from the westerly winds and an unkempt hedge of thorn and flowering shrubs divided the garden from the potato fields which ran down almost to the sea's edge. The glimmer of a fire flickered through a downstairs window and the green-painted door was ajar, allowing a widening band of light to stream weakly across the patch of bare earth which lay in front of the house.

Liam led the way, taking the other two on a roundabout route through the trees on one side of the garden where twigs snapped under their tread and leaves rustled in their wake until they came to the area in which the fruit trees stood. "There are apples as well as plums," Tom whispered, but Kate and Liam had hardly ever seen fruit until that day, and in the darkness they could not tell which was which. They were almost weak with the excitement of their hunger as they stowed the strange things away in their pockets, so many of them that Kate knew long before they stopped picking them that they had more than they could possibly eat. With their clothes bulging they slipped away, back through the trees and across a bank scattered with gorse bushes between which deep layers of green bracken grew from a bed of the dry, warm fronds of earlier years.

In their rustling bed they nestled like weary hares or woodcock exhausted after migration, shuffling their bodies into the dead leaves and heaping mounds of foliage over themselves for warmth, for with the setting of the sun the earth was beginning to cool.

Kate bit into an apple, but spat it out immediately. It was bitter and hard. She had never tasted anything so sharp before and her mouth stung from the acid of its juice. She whispered to Tom that she couldn't understand what all the fuss was about, that she'd no wish to eat any of her apples and he could have them all if he liked.

Then she tried a plum. It was soft-fleshed and so plump with syrup that at first, unused to such a taste, she thought that it too should be spat out. But after a second, when the sweet juice began to trickle down her throat, she almost gasped with pleasure. She finished it in no time and quickly ate the other three she had picked. When Liam asked her if she had liked the plums she nodded, and then, realising that he could not have seen her in the darkness, she let out a grunt so full of contentment it was as if she were a dog with a bone.

She felt a hand reaching out, touching her back, and she turned towards it, invisible in the darkness.

"Here," Tom's voice whispered, and she could just make out the paleness of his bare arm and in his hand two more plums. She lifted herself up on her elbow and took them from him. He did not draw back his hand, but left it lying invitingly on the floor of their shelter and, when she had finished the two pieces of fruit and lain down again, she put her own hand on his. Without a word he closed his fingers around it and they lay in silence, breathing as deeply and heavily as if they had been running for miles and fallen to the ground with fatigue.

Later, when she was almost asleep, Kate heard the faintest rustle as Tom moved beside her and then, with breath as warm as the breeze of mid-day, his lips brushed the tips of her fingers and he gently turned her arm in order to rest his cheek on the palm of her hand.

Not far away a pigeon sounded, echoed soon after by another and, with the calls of the birds in her ears, she fell to sleep, dreaming of a day she would never forget.

But the night too left her with a memory which would never fade. A memory of the gentle touch of Tom's hands, which later she learned could change so suddenly when his world was threatened.

Chapter Five

The journey home would take almost three days. They climbed inland by Ballinaboy and Ballinahinch, between mountains and by streams and along stone tracks where a coach or carriage had never been. The wild countryside of Connemara was left to them in solitude, save for a few of their own tending the lazy beds in which the potatoes grew, digging blocks of turf to dry for next year, or bringing in the fuel already cut and dried for the coming winter. In the glorious weather they were able to sleep under trees or in ditches. The days were hot and the summer heather warm and tall and if, in the depth of the night they felt the cold, by morning the sun's rays soon thawed them and they rose and travelled on in comfort.

They had little to eat, but they were used to this. The previous year's potato crop had not been a bad one but the families who, even in the good years, could barely scratch a living on their stony lake shore were accustomed to hunger. Food had become their treasure, their store of wealth. They wasted nothing, guarded everything. From the abundance of the orchard they had raided, Liam and Tom had kept back enough of the stolen fruit to last the journey home, and there was water everywhere, fresh and bubbling and clear as the sky above them.

On the morning of the third day, after they had left Ballinahinch behind them, they came to a cottage of mud and stone where a thin-limbed woman eyed them steadily from the door. She enquired about their destination without seeming to offer a welcome, but when they told her it was to Lough Inagh they were going she gave them a few licks of stirabout and invited them to rest a while. They sat with their backs against the rough wall of her home and raised their faces to the sun.

"There'll be no good between here and your homes," the woman growled. "Things were all right as long as old Lord Craughwell was alive. He'd never have done this to us. But he lost everything he had trying to help his tenants these last few years. Now some bastard cousin in Dublin has taken over his estates and he'll do nothing for the likes of us. There'll be no charity for poor travellers like you." Her children clung to her skirts as she talked, trembling with curiosity, their grimy faces awestruck at the sight of strangers. There was fear in the air. The three young people did not want to stay and they waited only a short while before thanking the woman and making their farewells. But she had been telling nothing less than the truth. A few hours later, in the heat of the early afternoon, the sounds and sights of distress became apparent. First came a woman, weeping copiously, thin and nervous and with skin which, although burnt by the sun, was wan and yellow and sagging from her cheeks. She stumbled towards them, stopping to glare around her from time to time and whimpering nervously. Straggling after her came a clutch of offspring, ragged for the most part, and wailing piteously as they made their uncertain progress down the shallow incline. Some way behind them came a man, clearly the father of the brood. A bundle of some sort was slung across one shoulder. He wore only one tattered boot and he limped painfully on a crutch of blackthorn. His other arm hung useless at his side, bound in dirty bandages through which blood had seeped and dried.

In the distance Kate could see three or four columns of smoke rising from behind a dip in the hill ahead of her, and from the frequent glances behind them which the wretched family stopped to deliver, she assumed it was their home which was afire. The woman carried almost no possessions, a few rags of clothing under one arm and, hanging from her hand, a blackened pot in which food of some sort steamed listlessly. They had not even had time to finish their meal.

"We had most of the rent too!" The woman yelled as they drew near. "We had most of the rent! But the agent didn't want it, wouldn't take it from us! Jesus curse him!" She stopped and looked back at her husband as he stumbled towards them. "They didn't want the rent, they only wanted us out. All for a few cursed sheep. And our crop not even brought in." Her voice trailed off into a murmur and she sank to her knees.

Tom and Liam went to her and Kate tried to pry from her skirts the hand of the youngest child, but the boy would not relax his desperate grip and his screams grew so loud that she let him go. They stood helplessly watching as the children, seeing the cooking pot within reach and motionless at last, dipped their fingers into it and sucked the food from their tiny fists as if they were mice or kittens.

There was nothing the young travellers could do and, humbled by the shame of their plight, first the woman, then her husband when he caught up with them, turned away from the three; seeming not to want help, but to be left alone, to be allowed the dignity of solitude.

Liam and Tom waited for a while as Kate, hoping to be of use, but wanting also to avoid embarrassing the family, watched them reassemble and form themselves into a unit again. When they were upright, their bundles back in place and the children's tears dried, they moved on down the valley, to a land they knew nothing of, to some unfamiliar, unimagined place where there could be no welcome for them.

When Liam and Tom reached the crest at the top of the valley they paused to wait for Kate and in a moment the three were lit suddenly by a shaft of sunlight. They had not noticed the clouds forming during their climb and they stopped to gaze back at the view below them. For some time they looked for the woman, her children and the injured man, but the valley had grown dark in the shadows and they were almost impossible to see as their drab, worn clothing blended into the greens and purples and browns of the boggy heathland. As the clouds thickened, their faint shapes grew less and less distinct until they could not be seen at all, as if they had disappeared completely from the face of the earth, or had never existed.

Chapter Six

Tom was the first to scan the valley beyond the saddle on which they had stopped. It was wide and shallow, with several streams frisking down to its base and meeting in a series of waterfalls and rapids and, lower down, where the land flattened out and the heather grew taller on the riverbanks, in still, black pools where trout and salmon lurked. There were no animals to be seen anywhere and hardly a movement on the ground, only a rippling of leaves and blades and stems as a breeze swept down from the mountains which formed the basin in which the valley lay.

Patches of grass stood brightly green beside the pools and streams and here and there were mounds of stones, collected from the lazy-beds and piled away from the drills of potato plants which ran in lines on every available stretch of open ground.

But none of these sights caught Liam or Tom or Kate's eyes. What they saw, all they could see,

31

was the remains of a huddle of poor, tiny cottages, some of stone and others of mud cut into blocks or dried in handfuls on to frames of sticks and branches and padded with clutches of straw or dried grass. Around each cottage was a garden in which odds and ends grew, perhaps a cabbage or some other edible greenery, a few flowers, a sloe or wild damson bush, or nearer the banks of the streams a rhododendron or two, heavy with foliage and dull without its adornment of spring flowers.

It was only the cottages, or rather the remains of them, which held the gaze of the three young people. They had been tumbled to the ground, every one, and whatever part of them could be burned had been set alight. The remnants of the walls could be seen, flattened as if by a powerful machine, some of them falling intact where they had been pushed, others shattering as they fell, spreading out and covering a wider area of land so that they were no longer recognisable as something which had been part of a house. The fires had obviously been lit not long before. Smoke billowed vigorously from several points and fingers of flame were still visible in places, but for the most part there was only a smouldering of wood or a flurry of embers as a surviving bundle of straw caught fire and rose with the heat of its own flames before disintegrating to ash and falling back to the ground.

It was a scene of such desolation and despair that the three young travellers were speechless. Nothing so grips the human heart as the sight of a garden destroyed, a house deserted or a village abandoned, and when that garden or house or village has been ravaged so recently and so deliberately the horror is hardly bearable to an onlooker who can think only of those who lived there, who can only imagine their anguish, and fear for their future.

The valley on which Kate and Liam and Tom gazed was not unlike their own in its geography and each of them was struck by the fear that a similar scene might greet them when they reached home. Kate felt herself shiver as the clouds which had drifted in from the south gathered again even more densely, filtering the sunlight and dimming their view as if to ensure that there should be no witnesses to the catastrophe which had befallen the lonely settlement.

The potato crop stood green and lush on the land as if challenging the destroyers of the houses to explain their actions; the streams which slaked the valley's thirst sparkled on their way to the pools from which the people had drawn their waters; high summer flowers bloomed in riots of colour around the remains of the cottages. It had never been a rich valley, its people had not known any of the luxuries of life, but four or five couples had lived there, tending their crops and raising their children until now, after one morning's foul work, there was not a living soul to be seen.

Tom was the first to reach the houses. The heat from the fires prevented him from getting close and even without entering he was in no doubt that there could not be anything alive inside them. Liam joined him as they moved on, approaching as near as they could each of the ruined buildings and when they were as close as they dared go, standing hopelessly as the fires completed the work started by the landlord's men. The valley now lay empty, ready for the animals Lord Craughwell's cousin wished to graze on it.

Some way off, on a high bank above one of the streams, Kate stood numb with disbelief as she stared at the scene below her. The bank curved away under her feet, worn by the racing of the water as it surged past, and exposing an almost vertical sheet of earth from which small landslides hung, awaiting more rain to push them to their fate. Below her and a few strides downstream, a group of people huddled around two milk-cows which lay on their sides, one of them with its head half in the water and breathing awkwardly, on the verge of drowning, the other with its legs crumpled beneath it and its tongue draped on the ground as if trying to escape the throat of its owner. A wild-haired man approached her, gesticulating angrily until he recognised her as one of his own.

"Even the cows!" he cried. "They wouldn't even leave the cows to us! Ran them over the bank. There's one gone already, and the other," he gestured at the animal which he and his friends had been trying to drag from the water, "if we don't get her out this minute, she'll be gone too and then we'll have no milk either."

"He has his sheep already bought!" a woman yelled at them. "The agent has them all ready to move in, as soon as we're gone! And gone we are! We've nothing left to stay for." She began wailing and rubbing her face with her dirty hands and shifting her gaze back and forth from Kate to her friends as if she did not know which of them might be better able to help her.

Liam and Tom arrived on the scene and jumped down to help with the stricken animal. With a lot of pulling and straining and several loud groans from the cow they got the beast clear of the water and turned her over. But, even as they did so, they could all see the useless foreleg dangling at an angle and the swelling joint where the knee was cracked. The cow would never walk again and there would be no milk from a cow which could not graze the mountainsides.

Eventually the woman who had called to Kate positioned a tin plate under the bloated udder of the animal as it lay there and proceeded to squeeze its teats with vicious strokes, but no milk came and eventually, with tears cascading down her cheeks and sobs wracking her chest, the woman laid her face on the beast's heaving flank and closed her eyes with weariness.

There was no more the young travellers could do.

"Dear God. I hope this won't happen to us," Tom almost whispered the words to himself. "I know things have been bad after last year, but we've paid what rent we could."

"There's talk that the landlords want us out," Liam said. "I don't really understand it. We work hard enough, we do our best to feed ourselves. Would they rather we starved in order to pay the rent?" He picked up a stone and hurled it away as if he felt the need to rid himself of something.

"There are some who wouldn't mind if we starved," Tom told him. "There are some who want us gone. They want to put sheep and cattle on to the land. They have their big houses to keep up, and servants to pay and feed. They've no interest in us any more, especially when we can't pay the rent." He too bent to find a stone and for a while they showered the river with pebbles in the hope that their fears would subside.

Chapter Seven

"Lord Craughwell was never our landlord was he?" Kate asked Liam as they climbed from the ruined valley. The sun had broken through the clouds and ahead of them the track was brown and straight through the purple-flowered heather, but the mood of the three was sombre. They walked on in silence, not looking behind them. The smoke from the abandoned valley lay low and menacing on the horizon, flattened by a wind which had blown the fumes into a long, flat, grey stripe stretching eagerly towards them as if it had decided to pursue them all the way to Lough Inagh.

"No, but the woman said he's dead anyway. And now it's his cousin, some cousin from Dublin who sounds like most of the other landlords," Liam declared. "They're all the same, landlords. Most of them bad, except the ones who are worse."

Kate found herself staring anxiously ahead,

shivering with fear. She dreaded seeing signs of another fire, or even the tumbled walls and roof of a cottage, and her anxieties grew worse the closer they got to their home. It was late in the evening when they came to a high point overlooking their long, lovely lake and although twilight was settling around them they could make out the cottages easily, even some of the figures moving restfully at the end of the day. There was no one in their valley they did not know – most of the people who lived there were related to each other somehow.

But Kate's fears were not realised. There were no signs of distress anywhere and the only smoke to be seen was rising from chimneys or the holes in the roofs of the cottages. Everything lay intact and comfortable in the folds of the hills which led down to the shores of the lough. The wind had died away to nothing. Coots and moorhens searched among the rushes and trout heaved themselves about lazily in the placid water beneath a butter-milk moon which had floated into view. The scene before the three returning travellers was as peaceful as a painting.

They ran the last part of their journey as fast as they could, downhill to the water's edge, away from the wretched events of the day and the memories of the disaster they had witnessed. They skirted the potato beds and leapt across a stream which bubbled a familiar welcome to them. The golden light of flickering fires lit the open doorways of even the most miserable of the cottages and the smell of burning peat lifted their spirits. Kate found herself almost skipping with relief as she approached her home.

Tom came with them to the door to say his farewells and, as if he knew he should make himself scarce, Liam clapped his friend on the shoulder and stepped inside without a backward glance.

Kate stood with her hands tucked away inside the folds of her clothes, her eyes on the ground somewhere near Tom's feet, watching as he walked into the shadows at the corner of the house. Then she followed him tentatively, stopped in front of him and raised her face to his, shyly and slowly, until her lips felt his mouth on hers and she could rest her weight against his chest. For a few seconds they embraced then, without a word she slipped from his arms and went inside.

Chapter Eight

Many months later when the famine hit, at the oddest moments when Kate found herself almost overwhelmed by the grim extremes brought on by hunger, the thing that struck her most was how poor they had always been; how difficult it was to remember the exact time, was it a day or a week or a month, when they had slipped from mere poverty into starvation. Certainly the time of the famine was the worst she had ever known, but when you have been hungry almost every day of your life, famine is not so different from what you already know.

For Kate the past year had been little different from all the others she had known and on her return to the valley she found no more nor less than she expected. On entering the house she greeted her family and took her place on the floor beside the scrubbed plank which was their table.

Her mother busied herself at the fire over which a pot of potatoes bubbled.

"Is there milk?" Kate asked.

"Not yet, dear." Mrs O'Malley kept her back to her children. "The cow is still feeding the calf. There'll be no milk at all for another month and then not much unless we get a good growth of grass in the autumn."

"Dry potatoes won't hurt us for a week or two," Mr O'Malley attempted to soothe his family. "But we might sell the calf," he continued. "Then we could get a bit of bacon on a Sunday once or twice, and perhaps a piece of beef to fry at Christmas."

"We need a new spade," one of Kate's brothers complained.

"And I need a shawl for the winter," Kate countered. "Can you get me a length of frieze and I'll make it up myself?" She loved the feel of the coarse woollen cloth they mostly wore, and she had learned to sew too.

"Your mother needs a pair of boots," said Mr O'Malley, "and that pot, "he nodded towards the fireplace "isn't going to last much longer." He sighed and shook his head, but soon his face brightened. "And we're lucky," he said. "We've six acres. How do the others live with less land? Look at the poor Lynches. Only three acres and thirteen children to feed off them."

"And no cow," Kate agreed, thinking of Tom.

"No land for wheat or barley either," said

another brother. "I don't know how they survive with no wheat or barley to sell."

The O'Malley family fell silent at the thought of their neighbours' plight and Kate daydreamed of Tom's brown arms.

"It'll be stirabout tomorrow, so," Mrs O'Malley announced. "We've few potatoes left, so it'll be stirabout every day from now on until the crop is in." She brushed the condensation of steam from her forehead and grunted as she lifted the heavy pot from its hook above the flame.

No one spoke. Kate hated stirabout, hated the bland taste and the gritty texture. And the wheatmeal she knew her mother would use would be stale and smell of must. There might even be mouse droppings in it which she would have to pick out, piece by piece. Kate hated to work inside. She would rather be in the fields, turning over the earth and piling it loosely around the potato plants to keep off the sunlight which would turn the tubers green. She liked being out of doors. She was good at tending the potatoes.

The family's fire-blackened pot was drained and emptied carefully on to the bare wooden plank. There were no plates and no knives or forks. The potatoes were simply boiled and their skins had begun to burst. There was neither milk nor butter to moisten them. They were completely dry.

The biggest was taken by Mr O'Malley, then in order of size by each member of the family until everyone was served.

Finally, when one steaming hot potato had been set before each of them, the rest were fairly distributed; a prayer was said, and they began to eat, holding the food in their hands as if they were pieces of fruit, biting off a mouthful at a time. To an outsider it might have seemed an unappealing meal, but to the people of Lough Inagh it was a dinner like any other.

In Connemara in 1845 the weather was almost perfect for swelling the crop. The September days continued clear and warm and humid, and the ground on which everyone's hopes were pinned remained soft and almost dry. The foliage of the potato plants stood knee-high above the tops of the drills, the stems and stalks were strong and the leaves thick and firm. All was set for the winter to come; there was no doubt of that.

Around the shores of Lough Inagh the weather held fair through September, save for a brief shower or two which merely slaked the land's thirst and softened the ground a little. Such barley and wheat as had been sown was already brought in, and a good crop it was too, for those with the land to grow it on. But the amount of land given over to grain was small and anyway it was a rare year in Connemara when a family could keep the cash they made from selling their produce. Everything depended on the potatoes.

It was on a Friday that Patrick O'Malley decided he would wait no longer, that the threat of rain was too big a risk to take and that now was the time to bring in his harvest.

His land was to the east of the lake, on a gentle slope of shoreline which faced the afternoon sun, where the crops had always been among the first in the valley to ripen. With his wife and children around him he set out into his fields with two battered spades sloped over his shoulder, for they used no other tools in this part of the country.

Further along and up from the lake shore Kate could see Tom Lynch's family, all but the youngest two or three, out on their steep, stony three acres, digging and spreading their crop to dry, and she even imagined she could hear Tom himself, singing or humming as he worked. She knew which he was, with his open shirt almost hanging off him, his sleeves rolled up to his shoulders and the set of his head on his neck like a warrior or a boxer, always ready, always alert.

Her task, which she shared with her mother and her two sisters, was to spread the potatoes on the surface of the fields and turn them in the sunshine. The dirt on them had to be dried and brushed off, otherwise they would be too heavy to carry and too bulky to store. As soon as the spades had loosened the ground they had to be found; all of them too, her father kept reminding her, as there were always a few which hid from her eyes and could only be discovered by sifting with her fingers through the crumbled earth from which the spade might have raised only the largest or those closest to the surface.

By the time the mid-day meal was ready Kate's back ached from the bending, her hands were caked with the dried, brown soil of the mountainside and her nails were invisible under caps of hardened earth which clung like hoods to her fingertips.

They washed in the sparkling stream, standing bootless in the rushing water, dipping and wringing their hands in the current until the worst of the grime was swept away into the lake. They would not bring in any of the crop that day. There was no danger of rain and a night in the cool air would do the potatoes no harm. Another day in the sun would mean more time to dry off the soil and that would be good for storing the crop.

The people of the valley worked until after sundown, until the air grew cool and it was no longer possible to see the potatoes against the dark earth. Only then did the men lay down their spades and stretch their backs, and only then could the women and the younger children make for their cottages as best their weary legs would allow.

They were too tired to be merry, and the job was not half done. They had tomorrow to think of. They drank their water and ate their meagre meals silently in near darkness, with only the flames of the cooking fires, dying as the families watched them, to light their humble rooms and brighten the sunburnt faces of the harvesters.

One by one they moved to where they would sleep, for most of them mere strawheaps on the floor, each covered by a piece of worn blanket or a strip of sackcloth. Some of them twitched as they dreamt, others lay as still as if they were dead. In the cottage of Patrick O'Malley only Kate lay awake, quite still and at peace, but all the time with her mind on the distant sight of Tom Lynch with his sinewy brown arms and the tails of his shirt flapping at his naked waist as he worked his father's land.

She hardly slept at all, but she did not lie weary and her restlessness fired her imagination. She dreamed wildly as she lay there, of the things only a young girl can imagine when she finds herself in love for the first time. And in the dream constantly was Tom: in front of her as they walked the mountain from the abandoned houses, near her on the heather of the turf bog, knee-deep in the blue water at Ballyconneely and closer to her, touching her hand, as they lay side by side in the shelter of the bracken where they had eaten their stolen plums and slept.

Chapter Nine

It was almost dawn by the time Kate fell asleep and she was soon back on the beach with the sunset in her face and the wind pulling her hair, but this time, when Liam kissed her and swung her around, Tom did not ask if he could do the same. He waited until she had regained her balance then, with a smile, he took her hand and walked with her some way along the strand to the boulders where the stoat had been. There they stopped, adrift in the tense silence that shyness brings, neither of them able to break the hesitation which held them back. Kate, her eyes firmly on the ground, saw again the skeleton of the rabbit, and close by it the body of another, but no sooner had she recognised it for what it was than she was aware that the body was only one of several, of many in fact. In her dream the small, dead creatures lay everywhere, singly, then in layers, and finally in piles as tall as herself, and pulsing as if they were alive and full of some foul, poisonous liquid which would not allow their lifeless bodies to rest. Then the smell hit her, a putrid rotting stench drifting across the beach like a cloud and lodging in her nostrils and face so deeply that even in her dream she imagined she could smell it with every part of her head, her ears and her mouth and her eyes. It overwhelmed her and she lifted her gaze to Tom, looking for an explanation, but he seemed to be fading from her sight until, as the vile cloud enveloped them, his face disappeared completely and she was left alone.

She began to cry out, fearing for her life and her vanishing love, but the smell of dead flesh grew worse and worse until she was choking and coughing and she woke from her dream, sobbing into the pillow of straw beneath her head.

When she emerged from her sleep and realised she had been crying she put her hands to her face, remembering the sight of the dead rabbits and their smell and thinking she could brush it away. But the smell did not go, it hovered all round her as she lay awake, penetrating her skin and clinging to her as it had done in her dream. She waved her hands in front of her to dispel the stench but still it remained. She sat up to gather her bearings in the familiar, crowded room, but the smell was everywhere.

Finally she cried out in alarm, jumped to her

feet, and went to the open doorway. She could see nothing which could account for it.

Above the fields lay a thin, still mist, grey in the early hours of dawn, which sloped with the fall of the land as far down as the edge of the steel-cold lake. From the roof holes of some of the cottages wisps of smoke emerged and drifted upwards, remnants of the dancing fires of the previous night. On the surface of the water nothing moved except for a family of widgeon pulling streams of ripples behind them before diving to show their tails to the dawn sky.

Nothing Kate could see gave any explanation for the stinking air which she knew now was all around her. She blinked and shook her head, so uncomprehending of such a phenomenon that she did not trust her senses.

She stood staring at the empty land until she felt a hand on her shoulder and turned to hear her father's voice in her ear.

"What is it, child? What in God's name has happened?"

"I don't know, Da. I never smelt anything like it. I was dreaming and in the dream I thought it was rabbits, dead ones, you know, but I'm wide awake now and it's not rabbits is it? Or fish?"

"No. It's not. And it's coming from the fields, not even from the lake. But there's nothing in the fields, only the potatoes we dug yesterday and

50

the fresh soil we took them from. Please God it's not . . ." Patrick O'Malley wrinkled his nose in a greater effort to locate the source of the smell, but to no avail. He shook his head. "God help us if it's the blight, child. We couldn't take it now. Not with seven of you to feed. Wait till I get my coat and we'll have a look. Come with me."

They stumbled out in the half light, Kate shoeless beside her father and glancing at his face as he picked his way carefully across the patch of ground which separated the house from the potato fields, wrinkling his nose and sniffing the air and turning his head this way and that in an effort to locate the source of the stench. But it was Kate in her bare feet whose querulous voice announced the cause of the problem. Unable to see the potatoes clearly against the lumpen surface of the field, she trod heavily on two or three of them before she realised what they were. They were not firmly rounded as she expected. Beneath the weight of her light step they collapsed to a moist pulp, oozing out of their broken skins in a mass which at first she thought was the fresh dung of a cow, strayed from a neighbouring field.

In the still air, the smell which emanated from the crushed tubers rose immediately to Kate's nose, stronger than before and pungent with the odour of rotten flesh, as if a plague of rodents had died in the height of a hot summer's day and swelled up and burst their innards onto the earth.

She retched violently and clung to her father's sleeve. Mr O'Malley was silent. He asked no questions of his daughter and Kate understood without explanation that he knew what was wrong.

"Dear Lord!" he exclaimed at last. He stepped across to another line of potatoes scattered on the ground and picked one up. He tightened his grip on it as if it was a ball or a stone he was about to throw, but, as Kate watched, the skin broke open in several places under a light pressure from his fingers and the flesh, instead of being hard and white, was a pulp which he squeezed out to fall in lumps on to the earth.

Patrick O'Malley moved again, quickly this time, to the far corner of the field. He repeated his action. A second potato collapsed in his hand and he flung its remains angrily away from him, shaking his arm to clean his fingers of the foul-smelling mess which clung to them.

"What is it, Da?" Kate asked. "Are they no good?" She was sure from the smell that the crop would hardly be edible, but she did not want to announce her certainty to her father.

A shout from the door of the cottage disturbed them and they turned to see one of her brothers, Kate could not make out which it was, peering at them, wondering who could be inspecting the crop at such a time of morning.

"What's the smell?" the boy called, and this time Kate recognised the voice of her eldest brother.

"It's the potatoes, Jack," she called back. "They're rotten, all of them, everywhere."

"Get your brothers, boy," Mr O'Malley added. "God only knows if we can do anything at this stage, but we'll try. If we have to spend the entire day out here to rescue a couple of bags full, we'll do it."

"Kate, you run and get the spades, and tell your mother we'll not be in for breakfast, nor lunch either if we're lucky. Let's hope there's work for us. Let's hope there's something here we can save."

"But what is it, Da?" Kate asked again. "What's happened?"

"It's the blight, lass. The same blight that hits us every so often, but this looks like a bad one. Sometimes it wipes out the entire crop. Sometimes a few can be saved. But we must get the crop dug, and put away. It can spread you know, even after the potatoes are out of the ground." He peered in the direction of the sounds coming from the unlit house and stamped his feet impatiently.

He was tense, Kate saw, with a frantic look

about him, afraid to acknowledge the disaster he knew to be imminent. He cleared his throat repeatedly, he wiped his brow several times with the back of his hand, although he was not sweating and the morning was clear and crisply cool, and finally he clasped his fingers together tightly, as if by doing so he might steady himself on the newly-dug ground.

They already feared the worst, although for most of the morning they continued to work feverishly, directed by Mr O'Malley to different parts of the fields in the hope that some corner of his land might have been spared the plague. They dug at intervals along each planted row and sometimes they unearthed fine healthy potatoes, pale-skinned and firm-fleshed, which they laid on sacks and carried off quickly in case the contamination spread, but it was all to no avail. Once or twice it took three or four hours, but so pervasive was the blight that even the best of the crop eventually turned rancid and soft. More often it happened that within only a short while of lifting them the potatoes had gone off, "curdled", Kate's mother said, as she pulped them despairingly with a dirty hand, releasing even more of the foul odour to hang in the air like a poison and assail their nostrils with its stench.

By early afternoon they could no longer doubt that the entire crop had been lost. They sat

54

where they had been standing when the realisation hit them, Liam so close to Kate that she could hear his breathing and beyond him their mother, weeping and wailing by turns as she imagined the winter ahead of them with almost no food in store and not a penny saved with which to buy it.

Around them in other fields their neighbours performed the same rituals, relief and anguish following each other in turn as one fresh find after another proved to be contaminated. Finally, when every row in each tiny stone-walled field had been lifted and every fear-dried throat had released its cries and every eye had shed tears of desperation, the wretched figures scrambled back to their cottages over the land which had ceased to support them. There, in the shelter of their homes, they fell to their knees in prayer to the God who was now their only hope.

Chapter Ten

That Saturday night in late September there was no singing or dancing on the shores of Lough Inagh. Men wandered the slopes of their valley muttering to each other of the catastrophe which had befallen them, while the women held forth at their doorways or by the fires of their humble cottages. The young folk, aware that a disaster had occurred but with no knowledge of its effects, were silent in the presence of their parents, daring to speak only when they could not be overheard and then, unlike the older people, questioning rather then speaking from experience.

Well before midnight a mist settled again on the valley, drawing into its cool strands the last of the smoke from the fires as if even that remaining warmth no longer belonged to the people. Beneath the mist's veil moths and insects zigzagged while eels squirmed among the reeds at the lakeside, nosing the mud for eggs and larvae or the plump, pink worms which inhabited the water's edge.

Tom found Liam and Kate sitting on a rock at

which they often met, a broad slab of stone where three or four could sit at a time, beside a stream which fell in a series of waterfalls and torrents down a mountainside as precipitate as a cliff. From here they could see all the lower part of the lake, the flat, wooded islands which dotted it and beyond to the sharp silhouettes of the Twelve Pins which stood to their west.

As usual Kate sat between the two boys, warmed by the shelter of their bodies and comforted by their presence.

"There's going to be something said at the Mass tomorrow," Tom said. "Whatever, we'll be on our knees for a miracle anyway. My mother says she can remember the last time we had no crop. The worst winter of her life, she said it was."

"Maybe we'll all have to go away," Liam suggested. "If there's no food here we'd be better off going to Galway, or one of the towns beyond in Mayo."

"I'd go," said Kate. "If you'd both come with me, I'd go. Look at us. The farthest we've ever been is Ballyconneely, and that's hardly a place at all."

"Where is there, I wonder," Liam asked, "where we might be fed?"

"Dublin," Tom announced, his voice rising with excitement. "They'd never starve in Dublin. My father says he once heard a man talking who'd been to Dublin and he'd never seen the like of it.

Shops selling everything you ever heard of, bread, meat, milk, potatoes and apples, and servants all over the place, wrapping things and even delivering them to peoples' houses. We could go to Dublin. We'd live like kings in Dublin!"

"My father would never let me go to Dublin." Kate laughed at the thought of it. "He'd hardly know where it is even. I'd have to run away if I was to go. But I would. I would if I had to." She felt Tom leaning closer to her and she rested against his weight, feeling his arm and elbow hard at her side. She knew he would go anywhere with her, to Dublin or America or Australia, and Liam too. The three of them could go together. She closed her eyes and for a time forgot about the failure of the crop and the desperate look on her mother's face. All she could see was water, stretching away into the distance, blue and gently rippling and then, much further off, land and tree-covered hills, beaches, the banks of sandy rivers and row after row of big houses, and thousands of people walking the streets which separated the rows of buildings. When she withdrew from the dream, which she did as easily as if she had lifted her gaze from a picture, she realised how little she knew of the places she dreamed of seeing and she found herself eager to go, eager to live, to escape from Lough Inagh and the hunger which would strike when winter came.

Chapter Eleven

The chill air in the church drifted among the numbed congregation like a flitting ghost, lifting the rags from the women's ankles and caressing the throats of the men where their collars hung open. The children shuffled restlessly, silently cursing the stone floor which froze their knees.

The sermon seemed longer than ever in coming and the priest, seemingly unaware of the discomfort of his people, took his time, as if this was a Sunday no different from any other.

The people of the valley had developed a patience which enabled them to deal with their priest. Their overwhelming wish on this chill morning was to hear soothing words, to be told that the failure of their crops did not mean that disaster faced them; that there were ways in which they might be fed during the winter; that God, their God, in whom they had absolute trust, would wring from the skies a miracle by which potatoes or sacks of wheat or some other form of food would tumble on to their fields, fresh and healthy, to be stored in their pits or their humble cottages against the long nights and the cold months which lay ahead of them.

But as the sermon began, the words of the priest were the usual fearsome words, of honesty and theft, faith and faithlessness, chastity and impurity. There was no sign that the fears of the people would be addressed, that the women whose lot it was to feed their families would be comforted or that advice would be given on how to face the struggle which lay ahead. Instead of dreams of potatoes and wheat and even bacon, there was hellfire and guilt for the sinners, the rogues, the doubters and the impure.

It was not until the sermon was almost finished that the failure of the crop was mentioned, and at last the people realised why the priest had taken so long to arrive at the subject. He had no solution to offer, no words of comfort. He was an old man. He had seen famine before. With no means of helping his flock he could say nothing, do nothing, hope for nothing, and if the threat to their physical existence would prove too much for them, then at least, if he did his job well enough, their souls might still be acceptable to the God who had allowed the catastrophe to happen. There was no message of hope.

The congregation listened as intently as they did each Sunday. Their church had no money of course. They could not rely on the church for help, but still, trembling in their worn boots or their bare feet or on their raw, reddened knees, there must be something to be done, they thought. Surely the government in London will feed us, even if the parishes could not. There would be no famine in London, they knew. England was overflowing with food. The English, they reassured themselves, would come to Ireland's aid.

And help was needed soon. Here they were at the beginning of winter, with the new crop failed and their bins and pits empty of the old. None of them had any stores which would last more than a week or two. And if there were no potatoes, what else was there? What could they eat? They knew near to nothing of any food but potatoes and stirabout.

The potatoes they grew were theirs to keep, unless they had enough left over to sell, while the wheat or oats, for those lucky enough to have land to grow them, went mostly to the landlords, sometimes in settlement of rent but usually in repayment of some debt or borrowing incurred to repair a cottage or buy a cow or a few clothes. Some of the people might grow a row of cabbages, others, like the O'Malleys, might have an animal or two, or be able to swap a few scraps for a bucket of milk from time to time, but that was all. There were no shops this far from the towns and such markets as there were had little to offer which the poor could afford. Whatever there was in the markets came from other small farmers, and what might have happened to their crops as well? If the potato had failed so completely in the valley of Lough Inagh, they feared, surely it had failed everywhere else?

When the Mass was over the people were listless, dragging themselves from the church reluctantly, with no answers to their questions and little hope to support them. Some of the parents muttered among themselves in low voices, trying to keep their fears from the children, but mostly they were silent. There was nothing to talk about but failure and in everyone's mind the thoughts were of what could be done to stay alive.

"Should we go?" people asked each other.

"Can we stay?" they asked themselves.

At the back of everyone's mind was the threat of eviction. Already the valleys were aflame with stories of landlords trying to clear peasants from their estates.

"What if we can't stay?" a man asked Mr O'Malley. "Where can we go? Who will help us?"

Patrick O'Malley had no answers. He knew

almost nothing of the world outside his own secluded valley. He and his friends had listened to people who had been to Galway town, they had heard stories of those who had gone further, to America or England or Canada, as far as Australia; they had heard mention of London and Liverpool, New York and Boston. But they could not imagine how such places might look or what life might be like there.

"Perhaps the government will help," a woman suggested. "There'd be plenty of food in London, wouldn't there? The ships could bring it in?" She was frightened. She looked about, seeking confirmation of her optimism.

"That would take weeks," Tom Lynch's mother spoke up, surrounded by her family. "We can't wait that long. We need food today, now. We can't wait." Her eyes sought comfort from the faces of her neighbours.

"Yes!" Another woman yelled. "We've nothing left. What will we eat tomorrow?" she screamed at her husband. Children clustered all around them, the oldest Kate's age, and they stared up at their mother as if she was mad. "We've nothing!" she screamed again. "The crop was due in yesterday, but it can't be eaten! I'd kept back just enough to last us till today. What am I to give them now?" She wailed and waved a despairing hand at her family. As if she thought it would help, she tore her ragged black bonnet from her head and threw it to the ground, stamping on it violently until it could hardly be seen against the dust.

"And this smell!" she continued, when her hat had completely disappeared. "Take me away from the smell! Isn't it enough to have no crop without having this stench in our faces to remind us of it!" She fell to her knees, dragging her fingers through the earth as if she might find something there to harvest.

Her husband tried to lift her to her feet, but she did not want to be helped. Eventually she collapsed completely, lying full-length on the ground, kicking feebly and whimpering like a child.

Kate could not take her eyes from the prostrate woman, wanting to help her, but unsure of what she could do and all the time wondering how her own mother could remain so calm in the face of such adversity. Mrs O'Malley held firm to her husband's arm, but she too had stopped to look at the mad, frantic creature on the ground, and pity overwhelmed her. She let go her husband and went to the woman, kneeling beside her and pulling gently at her shoulders until she began to soften her wails and rub her eyes with muddied hands.

"We must all see what we have," Mrs

O'Malley told her. "There'll be potatoes to be had from somewhere, I'm sure. We've a few still ourselves from last season, and we've some greens too. And the cows are still able to graze, so there'll be milk." She looked around her at a few other couples who had gathered and nodded at them. "If we all help each other we'll be able to get through. Some of us must have a little we can spare, mustn't we?"

Liam, standing beside his sister, shook his head and Kate felt his hand on her arm. There had been stories the previous day that the high land might be all right, that it was the nearness of the lake and the damper soil which encouraged the blight. But now they all knew better. To one side of them the mountain rose steeply from the valley floor. On the lower levels, where the land was almost flat and close to the lake, not a drill remained unturned and the putrid potatoes lay everywhere, like the stars of the milky way against the dark background of the soil. And higher up, even on land so steep that it seemed a man could not even stand on it let alone farm it, the crop had been tested too, and here also the blight had hit. The ground was littered with potatoes which the people could see even from a distance. But none of them had been taken away, nothing could be done with them. They would be left where they lay, to decompose, until they rotted completely and vanished into the ground with their frail skins, their pulpy flesh and their putrid stench.

"There'll be nothing to share," Liam whispered. "We'll be lucky to keep ourselves alive." He started walking, with Kate beside him and the rest of the family looking after them, knowing he was right, but afraid to admit it.

Chapter Twelve

On Sir George Gerard's estate, which ran from Roundstone across to Lough Inagh and Maam Cross, the last day of October was rent day. It had always been rent day. It suited the tenants as it gave them time to harvest whatever crops they had sown and sell them or hand them over to Sir George's agent to settle their dues. Like many of the landlords in Connemara, Sir George hardly knew his estate. He had visited it only once in his life and not more than a handful of his tenants would have recognised him if he had arrived there in person. His business affairs were handled by an agent whose duty it was to collect as much rent as possible from Sir George's tenants.

Most of the time Mr Blackstaff, the agent, would wait in his office and the tenants would go before him, one at a time, with any remaining cash they had saved from selling their few bags of wheat or barley to one of the grain merchants who scoured the country each autumn. Or they could bring their crop with them, to be passed to one of the agent's men who would weigh it and inform Mr Blackstaff of its value which would then be put against the rent.

Blackstaff was not the worst agent in Connemara, but he had neither sought nor won favour among the tenants. As a young man he had come west from County Down. He had known no one in the district when he arrived and, even after twenty-seven years, his only friends, apart from his own family and some of the other agents in the area, were a vicar or two, a police officer, and a handful of tradesmen who lived in the bigger towns nearby. He still looked on Galway as a wild, foreign country and its people as strangers. Indeed, after twenty-seven years he could still not speak more than a few dozen words of their strange, throaty language and, for their part, few of them could or would converse with him in English and then on only the most routine of business matters.

His men, three or four of them, were a surly bunch who, because of their proximity in social class to the tenants, behaved more cruelly to them then Blackstaff himself considered necessary, but he tolerated their behaviour. Firm treatment was what the peasants needed, the agent told himself, and he permitted his men to be as firm as they wished.

During October a despairing idleness had spread among the people of Lough Inagh. Instead of growing closer to each other in the face of the disaster which confronted them, they seemed to withdraw into their own families, often not leaving their houses for days on end and scrimping with what little food they could find.

Some, most often those with fewer children and therefore more likely to have been able to keep back some of their precious supplies from the previous year's crop, had small amounts to spare. Of these, some helped their less fortunate neighbours while others slipped from the valley with their well-filled sacks and sold their surpluses for cash which the landlords would never see.

Among those with nothing were the Lynches. Tom had five brothers and seven sisters, most of them younger than himself, and the family had less then three acres of high, stony land on which to support themselves. It had always been a struggle keeping back enough food for the summer months while they waited for the new crop to come in and, in the autumn of 1845, the situation quickly became hopeless. Within a week of the failure of the crops Mrs Lynch found herself facing her husband and thirteen hungry children with not a crumb of food in the cottage.

By the end of the month, living on water and weeds and whatever they could beg from their friends and neighbours, they were already showing the effects of their miserable diet. Their tiny hovel, never a warm refuge at the best of times, rang and shivered with the cries of the smallest, unable to understand the hunger which clawed at their shrinking bellies.

Confirmation had come from Blackstaff that the rent was to be paid at the usual rate and on the usual day. He came with his brother-in-law, Garrett, a crude oaf from Toombeola, on Bertraghboy Bay. They had ridden into the valley early one morning, hacking from hovel to hovel. They could hardly have missed the signs of distress which surrounded them on all sides, but they made no effort to acknowledge it. Blackstaff reined in his mount from time to time and shouted to anyone within earshot: "Gale day is the end of the month! Rents are payable same as any other gale day!" He spoke in English, only throwing in a word or two of Gaelic from time to time as a threat to anyone who seemed inclined to pretend they could not understand him.

Women glowered sullenly from doorways while their children ran from his snorting horse. Men returned his glare with muted anger, but there were no signs of confidence in their faces.

They all knew they would be unable to pay when the day came.

"You'll not be allowed to remain here if your rent's not paid!" Garrett added. "The law's the law. You all know that! So Mr Blackstaff's expecting to see you at the end of the month."

He dug his heels into the mare's flanks and rode on, covering the whole valley in less than half an hour.

"I'll not be leaving," Mr O'Malley swore, and his oldest son tightened his grip on the pitchfork which had been leaning against the wall of the cottage. Liam lay sprawled on the ground nearby, the sun warming him, enabling him to forget for a while the hunger which a diet of water and vegetable scraps could not appease.

"Some of us will have to go," Liam said. "I'll stay if you want, to help keep those thieves from tearing down our house, or I'll go if you think it's for the best."

"There'll be no talk of staying or going," his father rounded on him. "You're an O'Malley from Lough Inagh and your place is here!" He glared at Garrett's departing back with as much animosity as if he was challenging him to a duel for possession of the valley.

Liam lay back and closed his eyes but his mind was not at rest. Tom Lynch and he had talked it all through, and Kate too. They would leave and soon, but only with the blessing of their families. There would be food somewhere, in the towns they supposed, and if they stayed, what could they do? They would be simply more mouths to feed and already there was little enough to eat.

It was to Galway City they had decided to go, the biggest town in the county, rich with merchants and trade, they had heard, and connected to Dublin by canals and fine roads. There would be food in Galway and if there was not then they could move on, by coach perhaps, to some other town, to Dublin itself perhaps, or even by ship to England or America. Their optimistic imaginations knew no boundaries. There was nowhere they could not go, no oasis of food and plenty where they could not find a hearty dinner. In the grip of their hunger they saw themselves seated at tables far grander then any they had ever known and more laden with towering plates of food than they had ever seen in the whole of their short, hard lives. The future was not something they dreaded.

To get to Galway was the only problem. They had not got a pair of decent boots between the three of them and the roads of Connemara were long and hard, mere beds of loose, sharp-edged rocks, winding across countryside whose beauty was inhospitable, whose grandeur was bleak and whose charm was shallow. Its distances were a challenge none of the three had ever faced.

They made plans of course, but they were the plans of those who had never travelled with a purpose. They had no idea which route they should follow or where they might shelter if the hard rains fell. They had nothing in the way of spare clothing, there was no supply of food to pack in their swags of sacking and no money with which to purchase it.

"First we'll go to Galway," they told each other. "There will be streams on the way, full of fresh water, and orchards with apples and plums and we'll build a fire and maybe we'll trap a rabbit or catch a fish to grill over it." Kate shuddered a little at the thought of eating apples again, her mouth shrivelling at the memory of the bitter fruit, but she raised no objections to the fantasies of her brother and her loved one. They were all young enough to survive anything, healthy as yearlings and strong enough to walk halfway round the world if necessary. "And once we've got to Galway," Liam said, "we'll take a ship. To England, or Australia, or Americkey."

"Yes," cried Kate, "Americkey! We'll go to New York or Boston, on a beautiful white ship! And when we get there we'll find work, and we'll have a house, with a room for each of us, and real windows and two chimneys." She spoke as if she was familiar with the fabled cities of the New World, but in truth all she knew of them was their names.

"We will so go to Boston!" Tom yelled, "Boston it is!" And in his enthusiasm he pummelled Liam on the shoulder until he too let out a bellow of optimism.

"We must talk to Da," Kate looked at Liam. "And if he tries to stop us we'll explain why it's right. He can't feed us any more, our mother is sick and so is he. It would be better for them not to have to worry about us, not to have to feed us. They've enough to do looking after the young ones."

In his gloomy frame of mind Mr O'Malley could not argue with his daughter, but his unhappiness showed.

"It's only for a while, Da," she kept telling him. "Only a year, perhaps two. Then we'll be back." She smiled at him with all the confidence she could muster, but he did not give his consent. He was silent. He had lost the will to argue.

In spite of their desire to depart it was late October by the time they were ready to set out. There had been torrential rains in the early part of the month and for days afterwards the flow of water and loose rocks had made the tracks impassable. Then grandfather Lynch had fallen, cracking his hip, and Tom had not wanted to leave. No sooner had the old man recovered than Kate and Liam had to wait while their mother lay ill with a fever on the day of her fortieth birthday. It had been a melancholy affair. Mrs O'Malley was already showing the signs of her meagre diet and the sickness hit her hard just as she was trying to hide the effects of her hunger. Her waistline had reappeared as she tightened her belt to hold her skirts to her body. Her arms had grown thin and sinewy and the comfortable wads of flesh which used to soften the line of her jaw had shrunk so rapidly in only a few weeks that the skin, unable to contract, hung in folds from her cheeks while her neck was draped in ruffles such as Kate had seen only once before, on a turkey-cock.

The rest of the family showed their own symptoms. The girls' faces were finer and their eyes stared unnaturally large from their sockets. The boys were leaner and seemed to have grown taller. Mr O'Malley, only a couple of years older than his wife, had developed a stoop as if the weight of his problems was becoming too much for him to bear and his hair, which for the most part had retained its dark sheen, showed white above his ears and bristled out from his head, accentuating the thinness of his face and the weary lines which dragged at his eyes.

Chapter Thirteen

They set a Monday for their departure. They would stay for one last Sunday Mass and an afternoon with their families. Then they would go.

But like many a plan it was impossible to keep to. Blackstaff and Garrett came at dawn on the Monday with a group of their men, walking their horses in over the rim of the valley and waking the tenants by banging on the doors of their cottages with sticks and clubs. The sleeping people, weakened by hunger and tired from worry, had known they would come. There had been warnings. But still they were unprepared

It was three weeks since Garrett had told them the rents had to be paid, that they must find the money somehow, and when the people had complained that they had no crops to sell and nothing else to give he had silenced them with a raised hand 'You have three weeks! If you've not paid by then you must go!" He had not waited for a response – and what reply could the people have given anyway? They had settled down to wait out the three weeks, praying for miracles, but with little hope that their prayers would be heard.

On the morning of the agent's visit there was a cold wind, driving an armada of clouds low across the valley and spitting hard drops of rain on to the heads of the surly people who assembled to watch him.

He worked methodically, starting at the bottom of the valley and making his way to each house one by one until the whole settlement had been covered. Not a single tenant was able to pay the rent due and their resentment at the agent's businesslike approach to his task was equalled only by Blackstaff's diligence. His expression grew darker as the morning wore on and there was not a penny of rent paid over to weigh down his purse.

Finally, he signalled to Garrett who rode up to the neck of the valley. Even from a distance the people could hear his whistle as he stopped at the highest point. Then he turned back towards the houses below him and, when he began to ride down again, he was followed by a troop of six or seven policemen, mounted on sturdy horses and swinging a selection of weapons and ropes and tools from their saddles.

The group started at the first building they came to. One of the agent's men dismounted and stood at the entrance to the mud cottage. He called to the tenant cowering inside. When it was clear that the occupant did not intend to emerge, two of the policemen moved nearer, handed their reins to one of their number and entered the dwelling. In a few seconds it was emptied. The tenant and his wife were dragged out first, then their children, nine or ten of them, wailing and screaming with fury and fear.

As soon as the building was empty the agent's men set to destroying it with axes and sledge-hammers, smashing away at the walls and supporting beams until the entire roof began to subside. When the doorposts proved too strong they hitched a horse to them and the animal had no difficulty in dragging the entire doorway out of the ground, bringing down with it most of the front section of the house. In a few minutes the whole miserable place lay flattened, only its roof of mud and twigs and straw remaining more or less intact, collapsing all in one piece and covering the crumbled remains of the walls which once it had sheltered.

Garrett stepped forward bearing a torch, a thick branch of rowan, wrapped in rags which had been dipped in tar. It burned powerfully, giving off a dull, black vapour from its flaming

78

tongue. In no time the straw roof was alight and the heat from its fire was enough to set off everything else which would burn, the mud-covered sticks which had framed the walls, the planks which had supported the roof, even the door, a fragile raft of thin, ill-matched scraps of timber cobbled together as best the tenant could manage. The pile of rubble which had been a home to eleven people blazed away, sinking lower and lower as the fire's destruction reduced its bulk and in time levelled it to the ground.

Some of the onlookers were silent, others were mad with rage, but they did nothing against Blackstaff's men and the troop of policemen with them.

Kate found herself beside Tom and Liam, somewhere between the first building to be destroyed and their own threatened cottages. The morning had grown still and clear, the rain had stopped and there was not a breath of wind to draw the acrid smell of fire from the valley. Instead, the fumes seemed to rise only slightly before settling back to the level of the flames, wafting almost imperceptibly around the bodies of the watching tenants.

Liam glanced back at his own home where his parents stood guard. Blackstaff's men and the police numbered a dozen in all, not so many that they could not be driven off in a fair fight, but they were well-armed; they had hammers and axes, several wore pistols on their belts and a few of the horses had muskets strapped to their saddle packs.

When the first of the cottages was beyond saving, Blackstaff walked his horse slowly through the groups of tenants huddling by their homes. He leant across to Garrett and muttered in English. Then Garrett spoke in Irish. To all of them his message was the same.

"None of you has paid your rent," he called in a strong clear voice. "So none of you can stay here. Mr Blackstaff has been instructed to remove you all. If you resist we will deal with you as firmly as necessary, so I suggest you do not resist. We are armed, as you can see." He held up his pistol and fired a warning shot into the air causing the horses to skitter at the sound. "Our orders are to clear the valley completely," he went on. "If you go quietly you will be allowed to take your possessions with you. If you do not," he paused and allowed his gaze to linger on the flaming remains of the first cottage . . . "your homes will be destroyed with everything in them. All the houses will be destroyed whatever happens. There's to be no more tenanting of this part of the Gerard estate. You must all leave."

"Where to, Garrett? Where does Blackstaff suggest we go?" someone called. "With all the children," another voice added loudly as the agent tried to identify the first speaker.

"Ah! Lynch!" Garrett replied. He whispered a few words to Blackstaff then fixed his glare on Tom's father. "I'm told there's plenty of food in the towns. The markets are still functioning you know, in Galway and Roundstone and Clifden, and the government is to bring in supplies of corn."

"So we just take our fortunes to Galway and buy food, do we?" Mr Lynch retorted, smiling grimly at the men on horseback. "Does anyone here have any money?" He scanned the faces around him. "Does anyone have a penny left for food? Has any one of us ever been to Galway? Do our children have boots for the Galway road? Does anyone even know the way?"

Several voices cheered him on. Fists were raised in support of his bold words and his confidence grew.

"Shit on you, Blackstaff! Shit on you and all your gang!" Lynch herded his wife and the smaller children into their cottage and sat down in the doorway, barring the entrance.

Garrett ignored him. "Dempsey," he called to a young man and his wife and pointed his stick at their house. "Yours is the next. Are you going to go peacefully or do we have to burn you out with everything you have still in there?"

81

"We'll go." The woman spoke before her husband could reply. She darted into the cottage and in a few minutes appeared with a battered wooden stool, a bundle of rags and a piece of twine which served to hold together a cauldron, a fry-pan and a couple of stirring sticks. Her clothes were worn and thin, too light for autumn. Her legs and feet were bare and the shawl around her shoulders hung in tatters, so holed it would hardly have served to keep a dog warm.

Mrs Dempsey bade farewell to no one. She set off away from her friends and neighbours, her husband struggling to keep up. She did not look back.

Mr Lynch remained in his doorway, unmoved and unmoving as Blackstaff nodded to Garrett. The torch was laid along the thatch of the Dempseys' house and in no time its roof was ablaze. The agent turned nonchalantly in the direction of the Lynches' cottage.

Tom moved from his place beside Kate. She knew better than to try to restrain him. He walked easily, as if there was all the time in the world for what he was going to do. Two of the policemen stood off to one side, holding the reins of all the horses while the others stood with the agent's men in a line facing the Lynch's home.

He did not stop to take stock of the situation. Blackstaff and most of his team were already turning their attentions to his house. Tom walked to the horses being held by the remaining two men and pulled a long-barrelled musket from behind one of the saddles. It was cocked, ready to fire. He lifted the gun high above his head and brought the heavy stock down hard on the skull of one of the policemen. The other turned at the noise as Tom swung the gun at him horizontally, cracking his head and bringing blood streaming from his face. Both men fell to the ground, leaving free the reins they were holding. One of the horses neighed in alarm and Blackstaff looked around in surprise. Tom pointed the gun at the agent and pulled the trigger. He was less than four paces from his target, but the shot missed and the horses, loose now and free to run, took fright at the sound of the explosion. They headed away from the scene at a gallop, while their owners gave chase. With the gun still in his hands, Tom moved closer to Blackstaff as if nothing had happened. The agent drew his pistol from his belt. The tenants fell silent but they closed in around the pair as if to support the young man.

Kate gasped in fear and closed her eyes, but no sound came. When she plucked up the courage to look again she saw the reason. One of the agent's men, seeing their assailant approaching, had lifted an axe and run between Tom and

Blackstaff, making it impossible for the agent to take aim. Tom, in no way unnerved by this, dropped the gun and grabbed hold of the axe handle, pushing it away from him, pressing it against the throat of the sweating defender, slowly forcing him back towards Blackstaff. Blocked for space in which to move, the agent could not fire his weapon, but he stood his ground until his assailant was within an arm's length of him.

With the strength of a grown man, Tom took control of the axe and flung his first opponent to the ground, then, as Blackstaff fired his pistol, he ducked. The single shot missed him and he hurled the head of the axe at the agent's legs, knocking him on to his back with the force of the blow. Then he was on him. Somehow he got hold of the axe again and with one swipe crushed the side of Blackstaff's head before anyone could come to his rescue. Tom turned, aware suddenly of what he had done, and began to run. The tenants gathered round the scene of the violence made it impossible for anyone to follow and in the panic he was clear. One of the horses he had frightened earlier had stopped and stood close by. He vaulted on to it, scrubbed its flanks with his heels and spurred it to a gallop, his wild, curling hair flattened to his scalp and his mouth drawn in a half smile.

As he went he bellowed at the top of his voice, but except for Kate and Liam no one who heard him knew for certain the meaning of his words. "Boston!" he cried over his shoulder. "Boston! Boston!" he was still shouting wildly as he disappeared over the crest of the valley and it seemed to Kate an eternity before the thunder of the horse's hooves faded away on the spring of the emerald turf.

Two of the policemen attempted to give chase on foot, but with their horses far off, and Tom already out of sight, it was futile.

Garrett knelt by his stricken leader. The agent lay motionless on the grass, a sheet of blood gushing from an ugly wound on his temple and a bruise already risen on his cheek. One of the policemen placed his ear to the chest of the prostrate man, signalling for silence as he listened intently for a heartbeat. After a while he stood up, shaking his head and scowling at the tenants surrounding him. The bleeding appeared to have stopped.

"Nothing!" He said. "Not a sound. He may be dead." He shifted his gaze, taking in every face in the crowd.

"There'll be trouble from this!" He moved menacingly towards Mr Lynch, but Tom's father stood his ground.

"I had no part in it," he retorted. "I'm not

sorry it happened, but it was not me who did it!" He looked around him for support and the tenants growled their agreement. "Anyway isn't it justice?" he cried. "You've come here for no reason but to burn every house in the valley! You've come here to destroy us! What more can you do to us except kill us? And won't you do that too, if you have to, if it'll save you the trouble of feeding us?"

The sergeant of police ignored him. "Get the horses!" he bellowed to his men, his face distorted with rage, "before these pigs turn on us all!" He held his truncheon above his head in one hand. In the other was a pistol. In spite of his aggressive demeanour he was frightened.

"We'll be back," he said, leading his troop off to recapture their horses.

"Stay by him," he muttered to Garrett as he passed him. "When we come back we'll take him in to town. We must get our horses first."

Chapter Fourteen

They took Blackstaff back to Clifden later that day and by the time Kate and Liam left their home, almost a week after Tom's flamboyant departure, Sir George Gerard's new agent had already made his offer. But peace had not settled on the valley. No one who knew Gerard's methods had any doubt that his men would be back to evict the remaining tenants. The landlord was determined to repossess his land and the opportunity presented by the failure of the crop was too good to miss.

None of the tenants had enough money to pay the rent and, with their crops already sold to pay off their debts there was no chance of raising any. With the full force of the law behind him, Gerard's way was clear. In a matter of weeks the valley would be his, and with no tenants to impede him, his sheep would graze the pastures and his grass would be sown on every potato drill. In time, apart from the long mounded lines of the beds where potatoes had once grown, there would be nothing to remind the world that people had once lived and breathed on the land, that smoke had risen lazily from cottage roofs and that children had run and laughed and fallen in love high above the placid waters of Lough Inagh.

To his stick of eviction Sir George added a carrot. The new agent brought a message to the tenants. Those who left their homes peacefully, he promised, would be given two guineas each, enough to get them away to America or England or, if they preferred, to keep in their pockets until such time as they needed it to buy food. If they took the money they would have a week in which to depart. If they did not, they would be forced from their land and their cottages would be burnt or razed to the ground by a team of workhorses.

The new agent was clever. He did not offer the money to the head of each household but to each person over the age of twelve. That way, he reasoned, a few of the troublemakers, the young firebrands who might think it their role or duty to turn rough like Tom Lynch, might be got out of the way completely. After all, the agent reasoned, what harm could they do, penniless and without work in Boston or London or Philadelphia?

"Two guineas a head, Sir George," the landlord's lawyer had proposed, "to run every one of the ungrateful leeches off your land once and for all." Sir George had been in Dublin at the time, on his way to London. He had taken the lawyer's advice without delay. "I don't know how they survive there anyway," he had said. "They'll be better off making a new start somewhere else, where the land is more suited to their sort of farming. Blackstaff always used to tell me that. It's all for the better really isn't it?" Sir George had a horse running at Newmarket the following Saturday and he had no time to waste, but he had instructed his lawyers to pay for a doctor if Blackstaff needed one; up to five pounds, he had proposed.

He also instructed his lawyers to offer a reward for the capture of Tom Lynch. The Inagh valley formed only a small part of his estate and there were several other areas still to be cleared of tenants. It would be helpful, he knew, to make an example of young Lynch. There would be less opposition to future evictions if Tom Lynch could be brought to justice. So a reward of £200 was posted, and Garrett, already incensed by the attack on his brother-in-law, began planning his tactics.

When the new agent came out to Lough Inagh with his hard leather bag of money jingling beside his saddle and his offer of two guineas for every person in the valley, he was greeted with a silence less resentful than might have been expected. The people of Lough Inagh had rarely dealt in money, they had not known the jingle of coins in their pockets. Indeed, they could hardly imagine the value offered by two guineas, but they knew it was money and among those who raised their hands to show their willingness to go were Liam and Kate O'Malley along with every other member of their family.

"I have no interest in where it is you go," Gerard's new man said, "as long as you leave the valley. You'll not come back, either. Never! Understand?" Kate and Liam nodded and took their share. "There is a boat leaving Galway city in nine or ten days time," he added. "The *Mary Grafton*. An excellent vessel, and the captain an experienced man. She's bound for America and should arrive there before Christmas. There will be food on board and enough water for the journey." He smiled at the assembled tenants. "In America there is plenty of good land," he proclaimed. "I strongly advise you all to go."

He did not add that for every passenger from the valley who embarked on the *Mary Grafton*, he, Sir George Gerard's representative, had arranged to receive a commission of two shillings and sixpence from the ship's captain.

So the O'Malleys and several other families, all with their pieces of silver in their pockets, straggled off to Galway town to join the streams of hungry peasants thronging the streets who had walked off or been forcibly removed from the land from which they had scraped a living for as long as they could remember.

Faced finally with the choice of staying or going, their ignorance and fear sometimes overcame them. "What could we do in Americkey?" asked Mrs O'Malley. "With no money and knowing no one. Sure there might be land there, but is it for us? This is my home, Patrick. Connemara is where I was born. I don't know about New York or Boston. It frightens me. To leave here would frighten me." She shivered at the prospect and wrung her hands.

"The sea too," added her husband. "We're no sailors, and all the dear children . . ." With his words he tried to embrace his offspring, but he no longer knew how to lead his family. He feared the future just as they did.

Only Kate and Liam were keen to go. Kate because of Tom Lynch and Liam from a sense of adventure which grew stronger with each day that passed in the mournful city. But they could not persuade their parents and after a while they made no further mention of their plans to go. But go they would – of that they were certain.

There was nothing for any of them in Galway, of course. The *Mary Grafton* had departed without them and soon the season for sailing to America had passed. So they stayed, for none of the ships from Ireland was sound enough to face the perils of a winter voyage. As the harsh weather descended and the Atlantic wind grew colder and damper, they huddled in alleyways or hid themselves in whatever disused buildings they could find until the police moved them on. Then, with so little in the way of belongings that decamping from one empty house and moving to another was the easiest of tasks, they took the young members of their family in their arms, wrapped what possessions they had in ragged bundles, and wandered away.

They took turns begging for food, conserving their money for as long as possible, but soon there was no food anyway, not the sort Mrs O'Malley knew how to cook, and during the daylight hours Kate and Liam would walk out of town to scavenge for weeds in the hedgerows or among the livestock in the yards of the more prosperous farms. There they might find a few scraps or some edible vegetation which might be boiled up with a handful of grain to make a thin, foul broth which even the most careful cooking could hardly make palatable.

"I can do nothing with this," Mrs O'Malley

92

would cry as she stirred the contents of her pot, but her family had no choice but to eat what she prepared, and soon the pot itself was worn through, holed at the bottom and discarded in one of the makeshift hovels they were forced to leave.

In a matter of weeks they learnt to beg and steal, to put on the mournful faces which the poor believe makes their cause more plausible to their elders, or to look jaunty if someone younger could be approached. For there were others in the city of Galway who seemed untouched by the shortage of food, whose frames had not shrunk, whose shoulders did not stoop with the weight of hunger, whose hands did not tremble with desperation. There were people who laughed in the streets, whose well fed horses clattered past vigorously, whose eyes were full and gleaming, not sunken in their sockets like pieces of dried fruit dropped into a bowl of coarse meal. There were people whose lives were untouched by the disaster which surrounded them.

Liam and Kate spent much of their time searching for Tom Lynch although they knew there was little likelihood he had remained in Galway – even if he had gone there at all. They had no idea where he was headed after leaving the valley, but his final, triumphant shout, "Boston! Boston!" left them in no doubt of his ultimate destination. It was their destination too. They thought of little else except Boston, but their family would not hear of it. "Things will get better in Ireland," Patrick O'Malley said. "Next year there will be a decent harvest again and people will prosper in Connemara. The landlords will want us back, you'll see."

His wife would nod agreement and say, "Please God," whenever her husband voiced his now rare optimism and, encouraged by her support, O'Malley would continue.

"Why would you want to go to Boston anyway?" he would ask. "The ships aren't safe and the ocean will have you. Stay with us here, and we'll see it through together." He hoped as he spoke that he sounded like a man who could lead his family, but at heart he thought himself a failure.

They prayed more than ever. Not a day passed without some member of the family slipping into one or other of the churches in the town and with knees chafed by the floor they beseeched their God with a faith which was undaunted even by the tribulations which had so affected their lives.

It was not enough, Kate discovered, to pray for relief from the scarcity which assailed them, although little else occupied her thoughts. She was permanently cold and unwell and every day her stomach groaned with emptiness, but in church she was reminded more often of the purity of her body.

The Sunday sermons, while ending with a special prayer for delivery from hunger, were preached as if almost nothing had changed in the lives of the famished people who filled the aisles of the churches. For the most part, priests in Connemara were little better off than their flocks. They had no solutions to offer the peasants who had invaded the towns. The people came to the churches, the priests believed, to hear words, not of guidance or relief from their daily problems, but of spiritual sustenance. Sin was all around them still, the preachers warned, adultery and thievery and impurity of thought were rampant and hell awaited those who submitted to them. To the children brought in from the frozen streets of the town, crying with the agony of starvation, the words seemed irrelevant, but still the guilt was imposed on all, and in its perverse way it bolstered the faith of the desperate people.

God cared about their hunger of course, but he cared more about their souls, and guilt was the way to retain the loyalty of souls.

Chapter Fifteen

It was Liam who heard that Tom Lynch had got away. Believing he had killed not only Blackstaff but probably the two policemen as well, Tom had wasted no time in fleeing. But the news, when Liam heard it, was not so bad. A month after the O'Malley family arrived in Galway word reached them that not only had Blackstaff not died, nor had either of the injured policemen. Sir George, however, was undeterred. The hunt for the boy, which was already widespread, went on as if he was a murderer. A man whom Liam had got to know in the streets had garbled the news to him, but the man was old and enfeebled by drink, there was no knowing if he spoke the truth. Sir George Gerard, the man had said, had offered a very generous reward, and Tom Lynch, who everyone had expected to make for Galway, had had to flee further south.

"A good-looking young fella, yes," said Liam's informant, "and his name wasn't Gallagher either." He had hoped for a whiskey or even a bite of food, but Liam had nothing to offer. "I met him two or three times you see," the man went on, "and well I know I drink a little too much but I've a memory still." He nodded his head in agreement with his claim. "The first time we talked he told me he was from Lough Inagh and his name was Lynch. Then, a few days later (by then I'd heard about the agent being attacked), I came across him in the street, just there, only a few steps away." He pointed towards a busy corner where a grey pony stood between the shafts of a trap, its head buried in a nosebag, "and all of a sudden he's calling himself Gallagher and he's not from Lough Inagh at all, he's from Tuam or Athenry, he says, and he's headed for Limerick!" The old fellow shook his head, "and he was looking worried too. Poor boy." He stopped a passer-by to scrounge a plug of tobacco, but his plea was ignored. "I thought at the time," said the man in a confidential whisper, "that the police were on to him. I guessed he was on the run."

But that week a boat had left Limerick for Liverpool, Liam discovered, and no one had seen Tom Lynch since.

Kate knew though. She had no doubt about where he was going. She took Liam with her to the harbour and there, in spite of their fear of the wintry ocean, they enquired about a boat to Boston.

The *Mary Grafton* was nowhere to be seen, but the price of a passage was still two guineas and a couple of boats were set to sail before the year was out.

All their money had long gone of course. After a few weeks on the streets of Galway, the younger members of the O'Malley family, those who could not understand that starvation was something not to be fought but to become accustomed to, could not keep themselves from crying with cold and weakness. They would stare at their mother for hours with uncomprehending eyes, waiting for food which was not there and howling with an agony which was as real as if a lion or a bear had gouged their stomachs. At the sound of their cries Liam and Kate had not hesitated. Their precious silver coins had gone to their mother and soon disappeared into the palms of those in the markets who still had food to sell.

Soon Liam's health too began to fail. He coughed during the nights and spent several hours each day pale and cold, stretched on the ground in an attempt to rest. Kate knew they must leave soon and she took her brother again to the stone quays of the harbour.

But the agents for the ships had no time for

the entreaties of those who could not pay. The quays were full of people wanting to get away and few among them had a penny to put towards the fare. They thronged the gangways and called out to anyone they could see on board, their gaunt faces lifted in vain to those they thought might be able to help them.

Some could board the vessels though. There were those only recently dispossessed of their homes with the landlords' money still warm in their pockets, and others, richer or more frugal perhaps, who had the fare themselves. For the rest, such as Kate and her brother, there was nothing to do but turn back and hope for a miracle. But in the winter of that year there were few miracles in Galway, so Liam and Kate O'Malley remained with their family, buoyed only by their father's sporadic optimism and fed on little more than the love of their mother.

Christmas came and went uncelebrated. It was a time more dreadful than most people would care to remember. Despair was the only expression to be seen on their faces and, on the rare occasions when food appeared, whether for sale or to be given away as charity, riots broke out. Women who had been the best of friends would claw each other aside in their frenzy to get what they could for their children. Men would block the narrow laneways, even to those they had known from childhood, to ensure that no one could interfere with the purchase or theft of whatever was available to take back to their families' empty pots.

The days stretched into weeks and the months into a year. For the poor Galway became a hell without warmth, a city without a heart, nothing more than a place in which to die. From time to time attempts were made by some of the less unfortunate to alleviate the situation, but for the most part too little was done and too late.

There was little point in begging, Kate began to notice, as the flood of beggars exceeded by far the number of those who could give. Yet some tried to help. On a wet night in early September when summer had been forgotten, a pair of well-dressed women approached Mrs O'Malley as she huddled with Kate and three of the younger children in a ruined building. The women spoke no Irish but by their gestures Kate realised they wanted to be followed. She went with them, one of them even sheltering her with an umbrella as they walked. They came to a disused shop around which a crowd had gathered. Its door was open, its windows were lit by a pair of oil lamps and from its dark interior came the almost forgotten smell of food. Kate shook her head at the women leading her. "I've no money," she said. "I can't pay you."

But the women did not understand her and one of them took her arm and pulled her inside. A man standing at a table poured mugs of hot soup from a tall, steaming pot. He passed one to Kate and from a plate one of the women took a thick slice of bread which she proffered to the girl.

Kate stared back at her, incredulous, reluctant to accept the food until a ragged peasant woman addressed her. "Go on," said the woman," it's free. They're giving it to us." She buried her nose in her mug and slurped noisily. Kate did not hesitate. She bolted the food as quickly as she could and as soon as she was finished she ran to get her mother. "There's food being given away!" she cried "Come quickly! It can't last! Bring the children!"

Two or three times some of the family were fed this way but there were so many mouths and so few prepared to help them that the soup kitchens could not cope and soon, as things grew worse, the government began to accept more and more of the starving into the poorhouses which they called unions in an attempt to lessen the shame of those who had to stay in them. In these grim buildings food and shelter were provided, but the rules by which they operated were harsh, and the only funds to support them were taxes drawn from those landlords who still had funds to spare – and many could not or would not contribute.

For the O'Malley family the poorhouse was seen as the last resort. Its bulk and its grim design gave it the appearance of a prison, and they could hardly bear to pass by without averting their eyes and praying silently that they would never have to enter its unwelcoming doors. In the poorhouse children were kept apart from their parents and all those who were able were put to work. Mrs O'Malley knew full well that once inside the poorhouse their life as a family would end.

At first, as the autumn of 1846 approached, hopes rose that the new season would be better than the last, that food would arrive on to the infested streets of the towns, but by October the only news was bad. Once again the potato crop, although smaller than that of the previous year, had failed completely and for the O'Malley family the harvest season passed unnoticed, as if the days had somehow been lost, stolen, or forgotten by God.

By the spring of 1847 Patrick O'Malley's bouts of good spirits had become rare. He spoke no more of his confidence that the potato crop could not fail a third time and Kate, almost unable to look at her father's lowered head and despondent face, realised that at last his wife's reminders were believed. The crop meant nothing to them any longer. They had no land to dig and no seed potatoes to plant. Whatever happened to September's crop, they would still be hungry.

Most of the children had fallen sick during the winter, coughing slime from their chests as if those frail cavities were homes to strange, primitive life forms rather than to human hearts and souls. Liam spent most of the spring tucked away in the shelter of a dry-stone wall against which his father had leant some sticks to support a roof of torn canvas. Beneath this depressing shelter the young man fought for his life, his body covered in sores, always hungry and unable to move. It was not until the weather turned for the better that he seemed to draw life from the sun's heat and by early May he was able to sit and in time walk, leaning on the arm of his adoring sister.

But while Liam recovered his strength, the youngest O'Malley, Paidraig, died, a few weeks short of his fourth birthday. He had always been a feeble child and, when the sickness of hunger came, it swept over him like flames in a bundle of kindling, carrying him off as easily as if he were nothing more than a wisp of smoke. They laid his body in a ditch, as the cemetery was full, and covered it with stones to keep the dogs of the city from digging it up.

It was this final tragedy which caused Mrs O'Malley to announce her intention of moving into the poorhouse. She had put off the decision for as long as she could, knowing that the children would be taken from her, but what else could she do? she cried. They could not feed themselves by foraging for scraps and begging. If they stayed out of the poorhouse they would all surely follow their brother to a grave in the ditch. At least the poorhouse had a roof and food twice a day, she said, setting off at the head of her family – all except for Liam and Kate who would not go with her.

It was evening when the ragged group arrived at the poorhouse door. The sky was a cloudless blue, tinged by the sunset to a drear purple. A wind had sprung up from the west, cold and laden with damp, to settle on their faces and rags and their matted hair.

Defeated, Patrick O'Malley knocked on the massive wooden door. The building looked, he thought, a soulless hostel, too fearsome to be a place of refuge. A peep-hole slid open through which they were spied on by a small bloodshot eye.

"Yes?" said a voice in English.

"We want to come in." Mrs O'Malley held her two youngest children in her arms and positioned herself to make them visible.

Another eye appeared and a different voice spoke, this time in Irish.

"You're too late," said the new voice. "We're full."

"We've nowhere else," pleaded Mrs O'Malley. "We've eaten nothing for two days. My youngest died this morning and the others won't last the week without food." She did not have the strength to hold even the younger children up any longer. She lowered them to the ground where they began to cry.

"We must have food." This time her husband spoke to the peep-hole. "We're good workers all of us. If we're fed we'll work well." He tried to raise his voice in order to sound enthusiastic.

"We're full. We haven't enough food for those already here. You can't come in." There was neither hostility nor a trace of sympathy in the bodiless voice.

"But the union has to look after us," Mr O'Malley began. "You can't turn us . . ." He was not allowed to finish his sentence.

"You can't come in. No one is coming in until a few of them have died and there's room for others." The eye disappeared as its owner jerked his head back in the direction of those unfortunates who might in time make way for others seeking entry. The cover of the peep-hole shut with a firm clack.

When the O'Malleys straggled back to the ruin in which they had camped, another family had taken advantage of their departure and settled under the collection of rags and sticks they had called home. They turned away and for hours they wandered the streets of the town, shuffling with the indignity of homelessness, tired and nauseous with hunger, until finally, late at night, they lay down where they stood, in the sheltered doorway of a well-kept house. All except Kate. She could not bring herself to sleep so visible and so close to the home of another. She wandered the town throughout the night, aching with hunger, stiff with cramp, and heady with ambition to get away.

Chapter Sixteen

It was after dawn by the time she returned to the house where she had watched her family settling down for the night. The stone steps were empty, deserted except for an elderly maid sweeping them with a brush made of twigs, raising clouds of dust so high that she had to complete her task with her eyes shut tight. For a while Kate watched her, afraid to approach for fear of a rebuff.

When the maid opened her eyes and saw the frightened face of the young country girl she leant on her broom and prepared herself for a conversation. "What d'ye want?" she asked, not unpleasantly. She spoke in Irish.

"I'm looking for my family," Kate replied. "I left them here last night and I don't know where they've gone."

"Six or seven of them were there?" The woman said, retreating back up the steps.

"Yes."

"Me mistress didn't want them stayin'," said the maid. "So we helped them on their way." She brushed aimlessly at a crevice in the stonework as she eyed Kate. "One's all right, or two perhaps, but once you get a family all together there's always trouble. Where there's babies or young ones y'know. You'd start feeling sorry for them and soon the whole house'd be theirs and I'd be waiting on them hand and foot."

"Do you know where they went?"

"They didn't want to try the union again, I heard the woman say. She said they'd tried before and been turned away." The maid nodded her head, agreeing with herself. "But my master does work at the poorhouse. He said he could make room for them there and he took them along himself. One of the boys said he wouldn't go and there was a bit of a set-to. Then he ran off, but the others went. You'll find them in the poorhouse I'm sure."

"The one who wouldn't go?" Kate asked tentatively. "How old was he?"

"About sixteen, I'd say," the maid guessed. "Just a lad. Your brother is he? Then you must be Kate. He said he was going to wait for Kate." She lent on her broom, enjoying the conversation now.

"Do you mind if I stay here for a while?" Kate asked. "In case he comes back."

"Not too near the door," the old woman warned her. "The mistress doesn't like you to be near the door. Here!" She winked. "Wait a minute or two and I'll give you a biscuit and a drop of tea, if you like. The kettle's on to boil and there's only herself here, upstairs in her room." She smiled as a look of surprise crept across the young girl's face. Then she stretched out a hand. "Now," the maid went on, "come with me, child. I'll make a big pot and you can sit with me in the kitchen. You look frozen."

"Won't your mistress mind?" Kate was nervous of such an unexpected offer of hospitality, but the maid seemed unconcerned.

"Well for one thing she won't see you, not at this hour of the morning anyway. She was out serving soup most of the night. And for another she wouldn't really mind you staying in the kitchen. Sure, isn't her husband out at the union half his days trying to keep the likes of you alive and didn't he take your own family there himself last night and insist they be found a place. Doctor William Browne of Galway may not like people sleeping in his doorway but he doesn't mind helping, not even if the help is comin' from his own pocket either. Come on inside, you poor thing. You're already too long on the steps listening to me. Come in and sit by the fire."

Kate felt her eyes fill with tears. In all the time she had spent in Galway no one had offered her a word of comfort, let alone a seat by a fire and a biscuit, and as the maid held open the door, beckoning her inside, she stumbled with weariness and slipped, cracking her jaw on one of the steps and falling into a faint with the pain and cold.

It was mid-morning by the time she came to, lying on a settle beside a log fire. The maid leant over her, holding a spoonful of steaming liquid to her lips. A plate of bread and biscuits sat on a table by her side. Behind the woman Kate could make out the figure of a man, then two men, standing together, studying her. One she recognised after a while as Liam, shabbily dressed in comparison to the other, and feeble, resting his weight against the wall, but smiling with relief at the sight of her and holding out his hands in delight at her recovery. The other figure was someone she did not know. A middle-aged man in a dark suit with grey whiskers and grey hair brushed severely off his forehead. Even in her weakened condition she noticed how clean his hands were and how white his shirt. He nodded towards her and spoke some words in English which she did not understand. She opened her mouth to the maid's proffered spoon and felt the hot drink burn her lips. Then the sweetness of the tea trickled down her throat and she felt herself come to life.

"Liam," she whispered. "I thought I'd lost you." Her brother stepped forward and squatted at her side, taking her hand in his.

"The doctor says there's nothing wrong with the pair of you that a couple of good meals a day won't put right," said the woman.

"And where would we get a couple of good meals a day?" There was no hope in Kate's question. The past year had left her incapable of optimism.

"Here if you will," the doctor began in halting Irish. "You may stay here for a while and you'll be in the best of health."

Kate turned to Liam again. "Where are our parents?"

It was Doctor Browne who answered. "I saw them this morning," he said. "I found room for them in the union." And when he saw Kate shake her head he put up his hand to deny the words she did not speak. "They will be looked after there," he said. "I know what everyone says about the poorhouses, but there is food there. People survive there. It is outside the unions that people starve, not inside them."

"I'll never go inside," said Liam. "I'd rather die."

"I'd rather go to Boston," Kate retorted. "I'm

not going to die, not here nor in the union. I'm going to Americkey."

"You've no two guineas to get yourself to Boston," her brother replied. "You've the clothes you stand up in, like me. You've nothing else."

"Now, now," said the doctor. "You've little enough energy for living without arguing about who is going to Boston and how you're going to get there. Let's get you well and then we'll decide who's going where." He picked up the plate of biscuits and held it out to Liam then, when she had gulped a few more mouthfuls of tea, to Kate. The two ate hungrily until the plate was empty and Doctor Browne motioned to the maid to fetch more.

"You can sleep above the stable, young man," he said to Liam. "It's warm and dry. You can take your meals in the kitchen with your sister and Grace," he nodded at the maid. "Kate can stay in the house. Grace will make up a bed for you behind the laundry. And I'll find a way of getting the pair of you to Boston if that's what you really want." He rubbed his hands together as if to confirm his instructions to the maid and her two charges. "And now," he added brusquely, "I must be on my way," but there was disappointment in his face, as if he would rather have stayed.

"Who is he?" Liam asked after the doctor had gone. "Why is he doing this for us?"

There could have been suspicion in his voice because the maid answered almost crossly. "There are still good people here," she said. "Some of them doing a deal more than the government too, although they've no obligation. You're lucky your parents chose to stop on Doctor Browne's steps last night, young man. There are others who'd have thrown them off without a thought for where they might go."

"Why does he do it?" Kate asked. "He's not one of us, is he?"

"No," said Grace, wringing dirty water from a cloth. "He is not. But he believes in the same God as you and me. He's a Quaker."

"What's a Quaker?" Liam asked.

"A sort of hard-working Protestant," said the old maid. "A Quaker is a sort of good Protestant."

Chapter Seventeen

During the time they spent in Doctor Browne's house, Kate and Liam visited their family each day, although they were not permitted into the poorhouse itself, and their parents and all the children, even the youngest, had to work from early morning until the evening meal. With the strength which flowed from the sudden improvement in their diet, the two young people had no difficulty walking the mile or so to see their parents, and when their family was free to leave their accommodation for a while they would meet. Kate and her brother would delve into their pockets for any food left over from Doctor Browne's kitchen and whatever else the maid could find for them to pass on to their family. For although it was true, as the doctor had said, that no one starved in the union, the occupants were always hungry and everything Kate and Liam could carry was consumed eagerly by their brothers and sisters.

On the fourth day of their stay in the house, Doctor Browne returned late for his lunch and instead of going directly into his dining-room he came to the kitchen and sat at the scrubbed wooden table where the maid was used to doing her work. Liam stood uneasily near the door and Kate sat by the fireside as the doctor opened his bag and spread a bundle of papers on the table before him.

"You want to go to Boston, you say," he began. It was neither a question nor a statement. His Irish was slow and his accent strong.

"We've no money," Liam interjected.

"Yes," Kate ignored her brother. "We would like to go to Boston."

"Well, the sooner the better," Doctor Browne said. "There is a ship in the port now, the *Juno*. You can have a passage for two guineas each." He looked at Liam as if daring the boy to speak. "And here is the money," he finished. "I'm told there'll be plenty of food and fresh water, but I've heard stories that some of these ships don't carry enough rations. You should take some supplies with you, just in case." He paused, his arms outstretched and open in front of him as if his generosity was something to be taken.

"Grace will make some hard biscuits for you," he continued "and some cake. The journey could take four weeks if the winds are against you, but with luck you might be in Boston in twenty days." He paused and fixed their eyes with his smile. "So. What do you say?"

"We might never see you again, sir," Liam said, "to repay you I mean."

"I'm not looking for repayment, boy. Stay alive, that's all I want from you. I'm not happy about the way things are going here. The English are going to turn their backs on us I fear, and if the potato crop fails a third time there'll be the worst catastrophe Ireland has ever seen." He raised his hands in a gesture of despair before letting them fall to his sides. "The sooner you get away the better. There should be work in Boston, and food. A smart young pair like you will thrive there."

When Liam opened his mouth to protest the doctor silenced him with a smile. "Please, don't argue with me," he said. "I want to do this for you. I have no children of my own and I am not a poor man. Let me help you." He buttoned his jacket across his chest and smiled at the two young people.

Kate nodded agreement. "Thank you, Doctor," she whispered. "When do we leave?"

"She sails tomorrow morning, child." He stood and walked across the room to face her, placing a hand on each of her shoulders. "I know no one in Boston who will be able to help you

116

when you arrive, but you are a brave young lady, Kate. You will make a life there."

That night, as she lay in her bed unable to sleep, Kate prepared in her mind the words she would use to tell her parents of her plans. "It is not forever," she would say, "next year you will join us," or "In a short while we will come back, Liam and I, and we will all go back to Lough Inagh. We'll plant potatoes again and everything will be the same as before. You'll see."

But when the time came to go, all the words she had wanted to speak had flown from her memory and she was struck dumb, clinging first to her mother, then her father, then in turn to her brothers and sisters, until finally, blinded by her tears, she tore herself from them and ran from the poorhouse without a backward glance.

Her running footsteps were echoed by those of her brother as they fled between the drab walls which lined the streets of the city. There were few passers-by to witness their flight and no doorways open to them save that of Doctor Browne. They collected the bundles of food and clothing which Grace had prepared and, with the maid weeping and fussing behind them, they made their way to the quayside.

The *Juno* lay waiting on the rising tide. Her sails were streaked and stained the colour of mud. Her hull was freshly painted in black, but underneath the shining surface her planking showed the signs of many makeshift repairs and in places the timbers of her hull had swelled ominously with rot.

A crowd thronged the foot of the gangway, young and old, some already looking as if the hunger would soon take its toll, others as healthy as if they had not missed a meal in their lives. A few carried bundles of food. Some, like Kate and Liam, had baskets in which a few vegetables rolled about disconsolately. Most of the passengers were accompanied by relations and friends and on all sides tears flowed freely. Laments rent the air as mothers said farewell to their children, and grandparents, realising they might never see their grandchildren again, beat their chests and tore at their clothes in grief.

When the time came for boarding Grace laid her hands on Kate's shoulders and tipped up her face to kiss the girl's forehead. Then she shook Liam's hand firmly. "Good luck to you both," she said "and come back one day." She waved once, when Kate paused and turned at the top of the gangway and when the two young people were lost to her sight, she lowered her head and walked away.

Eventually all those making the voyage were embarked, eager to go, encouraged by the calls of the crew and hindered only by the cries of the families they were leaving behind. Once aboard there was a rush down a ladder to the lower deck and a scramble for what were thought to be the best places, but no cabins or bunks were provided for the passengers and none of them was familiar with the workings of a boat at sea, so they had no idea which would be the best positions.

The *Juno* had been constructed more than fifty years earlier as a coastal cargo ship, but now, converted in the most rudimentary way for passengers, her hold had been cleared of partitions and a wide space beneath the sea-deck had been set aside for the ninety or so hopeful souls who crowded into the area. The floor on which they had to lie was made of wooden planks, rough-hewn and lumpy. They eyed their rag bundles uneasily and wondered how they would sleep. Even a pile of straw was more comfortable than the splintered timbers which they saw were to be their beds.

On the upper deck stood a communal cooking stove in the shape of a coffer. It was built of brick and encased in wood, with a grate at its centre where a fire could be set in an iron cage. Several families settled eagerly around its warmth, not realising that the heat and smoke of the stove, coupled with the summer sun on the planks of the deck, would soon make the area near the stove anything but a place of comfort. Now, however, at the outset of their journey, they guarded their positions jealously, spreading themselves as widely as possible in order to discourage others from cramping them in and arranging their pathetic possessions around them like fortifications. In the days to come, most of the disputes between the passengers were to take place around this primitive stove, but at the start of the journey it seemed to be the centre of life for the anxious travellers.

When all were on board and the crew were in the process of hauling up the gangway, the captain emerged from the deckhouse to address the passengers.

He began to speak in a language none of them had heard before. A crew man stood at his side translating slowly and earnestly, but the translator's dialect was that of Ulster, his accent was unfamiliar and some of his words and phrases were not those of the people of Galway. Nevertheless, they listened to him as intently as if he had been a priest.

The translator introduced himself. "My name is Axel," he said. "I am the mate on this ship." He tried to smile but his face seemed unaccustomed to pleasantries. "No one is permitted to sleep here on the upper deck," he continued bluntly. "Your quarters are down below." He paused to emphasise his orders and pointed through the planking on which he stood. "For your own safety the hatches to this area will be closed before we leave the quayside. They will remain closed while we are at sea except for two hours a day, depending on the weather. During the first hour male passengers may come up to the top deck and water will be given out. During the second hour, female passengers may come up for their water." He paused to look around him. Not a person spoke. "You can cook at any time you want while you are on deck, but not if the weather is rough. We cannot allow the fire to be lit if the ship is rolling. Don't forget that. If we hit a storm you won't be able to cook for several days, you may not be able to come on deck at all. It's too dangerous, and we have no time to be turning round to search for anyone who falls overboard."

Some of the women passengers glanced at each other uneasily. One of them spoke. "How do we get water if we cannot come on to the top deck?"

"We'll have to see about that." The interpreter replied without reference to the captain, who nodded agreement.

"And what about cooking the food, if there's no fire?" another woman asked.

"It should only be for a couple of days, three at the most," the interpreter dismissed her concern.

"And don't think of complaining either. We can't have any of you making nuisances of yourselves. Our job is to get you to Boston. We aren't being paid to mollycoddle you on the way." The pair turned and made their way down a flight of wooden steps to the passenger deck. "Follow us please!" Axel called.

In the darkness below Liam reached out for his sister's hand and found her trembling behind him. They claimed a place against the forwardmost bulkhead of the ship and together they sank to their knees, peering in the gloom at their new, unchosen companions.

"I don't like this," Kate whispered. "I didn't like that man either, the one with the captain."

"He's Dutch," a woman's voice came from beside them. "He told us he was Dutch when we were boarding. This ship used to trade between Belfast and Holland, but now they make more money out of taking us poor emigrants to Americkey and he can speak a bit of Irish, so here he is, helping us get away."

"I didn't like him at all." Kate pulled her shawl close around her and shivered in the warm air, already fetid from the crush of unwashed bodies crammed into the hold.

"Well, we've all got to make the best of what we have," said the woman. "He seemed friendly enough." She moved a suckling baby from one breast to another. "Where are you from? You're very young to be travelling alone."

"Lough Inagh," Liam told her. "We are O'Malleys from Lough Inagh."

"We're from the other side of Maam Cross," a man said, leaning over from the shadows, "and I hope I never see the place again. We had nothing there at all. An acre and a half of bad land and nine children I could never feed. We'll be better off in Boston. Getting on this ship is the best thing that ever happened to us, water or no water, storms or no storms. My children will have a chance of something better in Americkey." He nodded firmly at his wife as if daring her to contradict him.

Kate smiled at him. The man was old enough to be her father and she liked his confidence. "I'm looking forward to Boston too," she said, and for a moment Liam thought she looked almost happy.

A couple of children coughed harshly and on the other side of the deck a man cried out as if in pain. Then, as the sounds of creaking grew louder and more insistent, the passengers realised that their vessel was moving and a wave of cheering and clapping broke out, echoed by the tears and cries of the unseen crowd left standing on the quay.

For almost an hour they were towed towards

the open sea by a rowing-boat and a team of eight men whose yells and curses rang across the choppy waves which slapped at the *Juno*'s planking. Then Kate heard shouts and the sound of running feet on the deck above her and the unfamiliar squealing of winches, and all of a sudden the ship heeled over before the wind and settled into a long, slow, rhythmic roll as she headed west past the Aran Islands and on to the broad swell of the Atlantic. Liam and Kate, their minds confused by the joy of escape and the pain of departure, fell into a troubled sleep, to wake only when the smells of food and the smoke of the cooking fire wafted down to them and interrupted their dreams.

Chapter Eighteen

There had been another talk from the captain and the Dutchman, their neighbours told them when they woke, and supplies of food had been distributed. One pound of meal or bread for each adult passenger, and a cup of water; but no one had thought to wake the sleepy pair from Lough Inagh and for the rest of that day they had to rely on their own resources.

They counted out the rations which Grace had packed for them. There were three loaves of good Galway bread, studded with grains of wheat, but soft enough to eat dry. There were twenty or so hard, sweet biscuits wrapped in paper and tied up in a cloth, and lastly a cake flavoured with ginger which they did not like at all. There was a basket in which the maid had placed half a dozen carrots and a couple of cabbages. Kate had hoped for some plums, but Grace had laughed at the suggestion. "In June?" she had asked. "Sure you'll be wanting pineapples next I swear. If you delay your journey for a couple of months you could go with apples and plums and all sorts of things. But you're going in June and there'll be no plums I'm sorry."

So they divided one half of a loaf of bread and they broke a carrot in two pieces, nibbling the unfamiliar vegetable like a pair of young rabbits. They were not discontented.

Some time before sunset the hatch was opened and the men were summoned to the upper deck, then, as the women were almost beside themselves with envy, the men returned and the women were called up to take their turn. Kate was the last to go, waiting behind in order to speak to Liam before leaving their sleeping place and when at last she reached the water barrel she was told the day's issue was finished. All she got was a dribble in the bottom of an old tin mug. Axel, the Dutchman, stood charge as the water was measured out. He attempted to smile at her but he shook his head at the same time.

"You'll have to be quicker," he warned her in his thick, strange accent. He allowed his eyes to wander carelessly over her face before holding her gaze. "For someone young you took your time," he added. "I can't always look out for the latecomers you know." But he dipped the mug back into the open barrel and held it out to her, brimful and slopping on to the deck. "Go on," he shook it at her. "Just remember who your friends are, and tell me your name so I'll know who you are in future."

"I'm Kate," she said. "Kate O'Malley from Lough Inagh in Connemara."

"And I'm Axel," the man said slowly. "From Rotterdam."

She studied him as she drank. He was not a young man, nor was he old. He was balding with a few strands of fair hair tangled at each side of his head. His skin was red and blotched, with marks covering his face as if he had been struck down as a child with some form of pox. He was short and strongly built and he held his arms tensed at his sides as if he was continually on the alert. No trace of friendliness lit his steady eyes or his hard face, but his gaze never left her. He seemed to gulp the air as Kate drank the water he had given her.

"Thank you," she said when she had finished the mug.

"There's more where that came from," Axel told her. "Just remember who your friends are, Kate O'Malley. The water's mine to give out on this ship." He drew his lips back from his teeth as she turned away.

That night the passengers prayed. The woman from Maam Cross began with a chanting prayer, accompanied by her family, and soon the entire deck joined them. Not the prayers with which they were familiar, the ritual prayers of Sunday, led by their priests: these were prayers from the heart, prayers for the parents or brothers and sisters they had left behind, prayers that the weather would be clement, that their supplies of food would last the journey, that Boston would feed them and clothe them and shelter them and that one day they would be strong again and rich and would come back to Ireland, to the cottages and valleys they knew and loved and could never forget.

When the prayers ended they settled down to sleep between the gently creaking decks. From time to time, as the ship rolled on a wave broader than the rest, Kate caught glimpses of the sky, speckled with stars, and clear, save for a few wisps of sun-reddened cloud which stretched out behind the wind like threads of gold against the ink-dark heavens.

She was full of confidence for her future. Liam lay beside her, breathing softly and smiling as peacefully, she noticed, as if they were lying at ease on their rock above Lough Inagh. Nothing could go wrong now, she knew. In spite of its drab appearance the ship seemed to ride the sea well enough – they would be in Boston by July. She found herself imagining her arrival in the strange, huge city, and she found with relief that in her dream someone came to meet her. As she stepped from the gangway it was Tom Lynch whose face she saw in the crowd, Tom who strode forward to greet her, Tom whose arms stretched out to her, to embrace her, and Tom who held her safe after her long, arduous journey.

She allowed herself to sink into the daydream until the presence of Tom Lynch was as close as her brother beside her. There he was in Boston, clean and tall and upright and clad, not in the rags of Connemara, but in the clothes of a gentleman. He wore gleaming boots, a tweed suit and a tie at the neck of his crisp white shirt. She positioned him opposite her and studied his face. He smiled at her with gleaming white teeth. She swallowed, then allowed him to step forward, once, twice, a third time until he was close enough to touch her. She felt him put one arm behind her on the small of her back and the other to one side of her neck. His smile continued but now there was longing in his eyes, and she tilted up her face so that he could kiss her and her own arms slid beneath his jacket and enfolded him.

When at last she fell asleep Tom's presence remained with her as if the daydream had come to life, as if they had gone back together to their lives before the famine and his face was resting again on her hand, his warm breath caressing her neck as it had when she had lain with him beneath the stars almost two years earlier. Then, with the imagined weight of his cheek on her open palm she slept as soundly on the hard planks of the *Juno* as she had that night in the bracken not far from Ballyconeelly.

Chapter Nineteen

After a week at sea Liam and Kate counted their remaining stores of food. Axel had told Kate that the journey to Boston would take not three but almost five weeks and that the ship would have to ration supplies long before then. The pound of meal or bread which the Dutchman gave out each day was not enough to satisfy them and already more than half of the supplies from Doctor Browne's kitchen had gone. They knew they would have to cut down if their food was to last.

"We've no choice, Liam," Kate told her brother. There was a look of bewilderment on her face. The vegetables they had not consumed were rotten and she threw them aside. The other foods presented a different problem.

The bread they had brought with them had become hard and stale and every time they ate it they had to scrape from it the patches of mould which reappeared each day. The biscuits had crumbled in the damp air and were no more than crumbs which had to be sucked from the paper in which they were stored.

"If we eat it all now," she pointed out, "we'll have nothing left next week. If we don't eat it now, save it I mean, it will only go mouldy and we'll have to throw it away anyway." She looked at Liam for advice, but he said nothing.

They had exchanged half of the ginger cake for a couple of salt fish which neither of them had liked much and which had given them a thirst which only Axel's desire to befriend Kate had enabled them to quench. The food they cooked for themselves from the ship's supply was even worse. They had no proper cooking utensils; all they could do was to mix their ground meal with a little water, fashion it as best they could into a loaf or a cake and place it on top of the griddle. But most of the time the heat from the fire was so intense that the outside of their loaf was burnt black long before the centre was even cooked and in this way much of the food they prepared was inedible and had to be thrown away.

On the tenth day of their journey the wind which had followed them all the way from the coast of Galway veered around and took the *Juno* head-on, strengthening to a gale and bringing with it rain-laden blasts of air which sought every corner of the ship and lodged cold in the rags and bones of the passengers.

The captain gave orders to shorten sail and bear north and the *Juno* wallowed discomfortingly in the high swell while her unhappy human cargo, locked for safety in their cramped quarters, were left to lie in their own vomit, with almost no water and little will to feed themselves.

For three days the storm raged about them, at the end of which four people were dead; although two of the deaths had gone unnoticed in the chaos of the tossing ship, and a third, an elderly woman, had injured herself so badly in a fall that she died a few hours after the storm had abated.

When the storm had died away the burials began. Those passengers still able to stand made their way to the upper deck where the bodies lay in a row, shrouded in roughly-torn canvas. Kate felt herself shivering and she took Liam's arm as the prayers began, but her trembling did not stop.

"It could so easily have been us," she murmured. Her brother glanced at her but she said nothing more and Liam, shamed by his inability to be of use to his fellow-passengers, choked back his tears.

"If you go, I'd want to go with you," he replied, and they gripped each other's hands as if that gesture alone might protect and save them.

133

For most of the passengers food and water was now their only thought. During the storm some of the water barrels, which had been lashed together on the deck, had been punctured and much of the ship's precious supply had been lost or was too salty to drink. Such remnants of food as still remained had become mostly inedible.

The first signs of the fever with which the passengers were soon to become familiar now began to show themselves. Those with the least food developed a thirst which was almost impossible to quench even if there had been adequate supplies of water. Huge sores broke out on the bodies of the sufferers and their tongues swelled so much that swallowing was almost impossible.

In the darkness below deck it was not easy to see the signs of the fever, and often, when someone emerged into the daylight for the first time after a few days, the cries of alarm and fear were almost unbearable. A man would see his wife for the first time, gaunt and pale-skinned except for the blotches which disfigured her arms and face, and draw away from her in horror; while she, afraid of passing the illness on to her children, would cower from them, forcing them from her while all the time she wished for nothing more than to embrace them, comfort them, even, in some cases where they were not fully weaned, to suckle them at her flaccid breast.

After the first two weeks all but a few of the passengers came to resemble ghosts, hollow-cheeked, yellow and shrunken, with arms which hung limply and without strength and hands which could hardly grasp the rails which led them to the fresh air of the upper deck. Those who retained some semblance of wellbeing did so with embarrassment. It was not their fault, they thought, that they had come better prepared for the voyage, that they had saved more of their food or were better dressed for the weather. Survival was all that mattered and they guarded their supplies jealously, took their share of water every day and thanked God for their foresight.

Most often it was the small and the poor who succumbed first. The family from Maam Cross lost two of their number during the second week and even when the storm had passed and the wind was once again in their favour the mother had to suffer the agony of seeing the bodies of three more of her children tipped overboard. Then her husband, weak from a hunger brought on by his willingness to give his share of the food to the neediest of his children, died in his sleep and all night, unable to accept the reality of his death, his wife clung to the cold body of her spouse until she was prised from it by her neighbours and he too was taken away to be sacrificed to the sea.

Liam and Kate's supply of food ran out during the third week, as fever raged among the passengers. The pains brought about by the absence of food were so great that two boys, maddened by the ravings of hunger and fear, threw themselves from the ship during their precious time on deck. The waves swallowed them in an instant, as if the sea's hunger was as great as that of the passengers themselves. No one on board suggested the ship turn back.

Any sense of hope which had lingered among the passengers vanished as the toll of death mounted. Hardly a day passed without a body or two being brought up from the foul-smelling lower deck to be lamented and pushed overboard and every day the stench in the hold grew more and more frightful. No one was well enough or strong enough to clean away the mess of vomit and excrement which had accumulated during the lengthening journey, and as their energy began to fail, people lay where they could, on their fouled layers of improvised bedding, or simply on bare boards if they could find them. What supplies of food remained became contaminated by contact with the air of the ship, or worse, the possessions of the passengers themselves. Some were struck by dysentery, others by typhus, which later would become known as famine fever, and which raged like a fire.

No one escaped. At first it had seemed to Kate and Liam that the hunger was the worst aspect of the voyage but later, when the plague was at its worst, they too succumbed to the lethargy it induced, raising themselves from their resting places only to stagger up to the sea deck when it was time to treat themselves to the putrid water which now comprised their principal sustenance.

It was during one of these visits to the water barrel that Axel made his offer. He squatted beside Kate as she sat on the deck holding the mug of water to her lips. There seemed to be an unaccustomed tenderness in his gesture which affected her and she returned his intense stare with a faint smile.

"What have you got to eat down there?" he asked.

"Nothing," Kate replied. "We've had nothing but damp meal for ten days, apart from this dirty water. And they say Boston is still almost a week away."

"You're hungry then?" The Dutchman lowered himself to sit beside her, close enough for her to be able to smell him and for his stocky legs to lie alongside hers.

"Of course we're hungry." Kate tried to

137

clamber to her feet, but Axel's hand on her shoulder restrained her and she fell back to the deck.

"There's plenty of food on board," he whispered, "for those that really want it." He leant towards her and put his mouth to her ear. "A pretty young girl like you doesn't have to go hungry, you know. Come with me now and I'll see what I can do for you." For a second he let his callused lips rest against the soft skin of her cheek, but she moved away sharply, putting her hand to her face to ward him off.

"It's my brother who needs to eat, not me," Kate told him. "He's been unwell for months."

"Well, there's enough for your brother too, if that's what you want. Come with me now and I'll see what we can find for the pair of you." His voice was softer than Kate remembered. He almost smiled.

It was true that Liam was more in need of food than his sister. It was only with the help of Kate and another man who had managed to keep his strength that the youth was able to get up to the open deck for water and fresh air. He could no longer stand unaided and he spent most of the days as well as nights asleep in the corner of the lower deck which he and Kate had made their own.

By now the sores on his body were so

disfiguring that it was only through love that Kate was able to hold him to her. His breath had grown so foul that she could hardly bear to have his head on her lap and his hands had lost their strength. His grip had become as weak as that of a child.

Still she nursed him as best she could and in the depths of his illness her presence was the only thing which kept him alive.

So, fearing the ugly little Dutchman who sat so close to her, but fearing her brother's hunger even more, Kate nodded and pushed herself up to lean on the ship's rail. Axel's smile was almost warm. "Follow me," he said, with a nod of his head towards the deck-house.

The passageway they entered was so low that even Kate had to stoop. To one side lay a series of small cabins without doors, each used as a store for ship's tackle, bolts of sailcloth, or barrels of tar. At the end of the passage, the last of the cabins was screened from view by a ragged cloth which hung crookedly from a length of twine strung across the opening. Kate paused to steady herself against the wall as Axel pushed the makeshift curtain aside and entered the small room.

"The food's in here," he called. "Biscuits, bread, tea. Whatever I have you can share. Come in and sit down."

Kate hung back, afraid. She did not move until the Dutchman's face appeared at the opening. "Can't I take it away with me?" she asked. "Please. I want to share it with my brother."

"You can share it with whoever you like, Miss, but first you've got to get it. Understand? You've got to come in!" The man's voice was beginning to sound impatient. Kate was afraid he would change his mind. She took a step forward and peered into the tiny cabin.

Axel stood with a wooden box in his arms. He reached into it and pulled out a broken piece of biscuit, offering it to the girl. Kate took it and stuffed it into her mouth. She had almost forgotten the sweet taste and she savoured each crumb, licking her lips and running her tongue round her gums to make sure she had missed nothing.

"Sit down." The man from Rotterdam patted the bunk beside him which took up one side of the small cabin. He broke off another piece of biscuit and held it out to her. It was just out of reach and she had to step further into the cabin. This time, when she accepted the biscuit from him, Axel did not withdraw his hand. He slipped it under her knuckles and tightened his fingers around her thin wrist. He pulled her towards him. "It tastes good, doesn't it?" He

140

leered. "My biscuits taste good don't they. Now, how many do you want, Kate? And what do I get in return?"

Kate stared at him in horror, realising suddenly the situation she was in. But the taste of the biscuit filled her mouth and her empty stomach cried for more.

"Your brother might die you know, before we get to Boston." Axel rattled the contents of the box invitingly. "There's enough food here to keep him alive, to keep both of you alive." He put the box down on the bunk and put his other hand on Kate's shoulder, pulling her towards him. He leaned forward, bringing his face close to hers, and parted his chapped lips.

She turned away from him. "No," she said. "I don't want to kiss you." She bit the inside of her mouth. The box of food lay open beneath her. She noticed that it was almost full.

"I don't want to kiss you, either," Axel growled. "If you want food, enough for you and your brother, then I want more than a kiss or two. Understand?" She could see his tongue moving behind his cheeks. He was breathing so deeply she could feel the warmth on her face.

She was numb with fear. No man had ever looked at her with such cruelty and desire. He kept hold of her as she tried to avoid his gaze. The taste of biscuit in her mouth had gone, but her stomach had stopped its aching for the first time in days.

"That brother of yours, Liam. How much do you want Liam to live?" The man released his grip on her wrist and reached down into the box. He held up a handful of biscuits. "Sit on the bed with me, girl. Sit down here on the bed!"

He tried to force her on to the bunk, but she tore herself away from his grip and turned to flee, knocking the biscuits from his hand on to the dirty floor of the cabin.

She ran as fast as her strength would allow, Axel's voice following her down the narrow passageway. "Tell Liam there's food here for him!" he yelled. "All you need to do is stay with me for a while!" Then, coming to the doorway of the cabin, he called even louder. "You'll be back, girl! You'll be back! Or your brother won't live to see Boston!"

Chapter Twenty

Liam was delirious with fever that night. He sweated as if the air on board the *Juno* was unbearably hot, although they were sailing through rough seas churned by a chill northerly wind. He lay moaning on the pile of rags which was his bed and his feeble cries were hardly distinguishable from those of the sick and dying who surrounded him on all sides.

By the end of the fourth week, of the ninety creatures who had started out from Galway, fewer than fifty remained alive and of these not more than half could have been thought to have a chance of survival. Kate O'Malley was one of the lucky ones. True, she had lost the freshness from her complexion and she was as thin as a skeleton, but the fever sores which had disfigured the bodies of most of her companions had been much less severe on her youthful skin, and the gauntness which had shrivelled the faces of all those on board served only to emphasise the beauty of her jawline and breadth of her cheekbones.

She could think of little else but the Dutchman's advances to her and the box of food he guarded in his room. The pangs of hunger which had been temporarily alleviated by the biscuit he had given her had returned, stronger than ever, worsened by the memory of its taste and smell, by the feel of the crumbs on her tongue. She was maddened by the thought of so much being offered to her, and lying on the hard planks, conscious of Liam's pitiful condition as well as her own aching stomach, her refusal to do as the man had wanted seemed less justified.

He had been right to say that her brother would not survive the journey. Kate could see for herself how quickly Liam was weakening. She could hardly believe how someone as young and strong as her brother could have slipped so easily into the grip of illness. He seemed to sleep with his eyes open, she noticed, and his breath rattled in his throat, shaking his lips as he exhaled. She lay her hand on his forehead and stroked his face. "Live, Liam," she prayed. "Live as far as Boston, then we will be all right." She felt tears welling in her eyes and she began to speak aloud, oblivious to those around her.

"Stay with me till Boston, Liam," she murmured. "Hold my hand. I won't be able to survive there without you. Someone there will help us. I'll find someone. Perhaps Tom is there already. Tom! Tom!" At the thought of the name of her love, Kate began sobbing, and her mind was empty of everything except him, but she did not even know where he was.

Was he in Boston? Was he safe? She remembered the sea burials she had witnessed and against her will she conjured up a picture of Tom dead and she wondered if she would ever have to see someone she loved tipped so callously into the water. At the thought she cried out loud in fear. Tom must have made his escape in winter when the seas were wild and the waters ice-cold. Had he survived? Was he alive?

At the thought of what might have happened her strength left her and she toppled over, weak with grief, to lie beside her brother.

As the women passengers reached the upper deck the next afternoon word was out that they expected to reach Boston in less than two days. Some of the passengers attempted to clean up their quarters as though they could not bear to be seen to have lived in such squalor. Others, those with a few zealously guarded scraps of food left, consumed them greedily, confident that with Boston just over the horizon there would soon be plenty for all. Axel, doling out the water which was for many of them the only thing to have passed their lips for days, was generosity itself, doubling the rations, permitting passengers to come on deck as and when they pleased, even allowing some of those he favoured to help themselves from the barrel.

The excitement grew with each hour. A man who a few days earlier had seemed to be near death appeared on deck with a tin whistle and struck up a merry tune to which a few of the women tried to dance, lifting their knees pathetically and chanting with voices so weakened by hunger that they sounded like small children. Soon the sense that their nightmare was drawing to an end lent an air of exhilaration to the *Juno*'s passengers. One of the men began to sing, a boy joined him, then two women and a young girl. Miraculously the clouds fled the sky, leaving above the boat a vast blue heaven from which the sun's rays spilt, glinting on the wave crests, drying the sails, heating the planks of the deck and warming the skins of the *Juno*'s human cargo until the travellers could almost imagine they were well again.

The little whistle shrilled as the people joined in. The music grew loud and joyful and how they all sang! No practised choir could have sounded more sweet, no angels' voices could better have pleased their Lord; and finally, when one of the deck-hands stepped up, a battered fiddle lying on his arm and a bow in his hand to draw across it, all those who could still use their lungs burst into song as lustily as a group of wedding guests with a splendid dowry to celebrate. Airs they sang and rousing choruses, while the fiddle and the whistle played jigs and reels and the people leapt to their feet and danced and cried out and whooped merrily on the joyful deck and the dead were all forgotten.

For an hour or more they clung to their happiness until exhaustion slowed them and one by one they sank to their knees, smiling and tearful at the same time, their spirits lifted by the music, their memories empty for a while of those who were not there.

Pleased that the mood of his passengers had improved, the captain extended the hours they could spend on deck and those who could remained to bask in the sunlight and lean on the rails in peace. Away to the north they could see another vessel heading in the same direction as the *Juno*, her white sails set high, filled by the same friendly wind. At last, the passengers thought, we are not alone.

A surge of optimism swept the boat, affecting even Kate. Perhaps, she told herself, we can hold out until Boston. Perhaps I need not go with Axel to the cabin. Perhaps we are safe. But the merest glance at her brother told her that he would not live more than another day without food. Kate knew she must act.

Liam was among those who could no longer make the climb from the passengers' quarters. He spent the days so near death in the dark squalor of the hold that even his trembling seemed to tire him. Then, with little more than a day to go and Boston so close they could almost smell its nearness, the wind turned against the *Juno* again and strengthened so that once more they had to bear off course, away from the city which was to be their salvation. Several days would be added to their journey, they were told. Kate's mind was made up.

When Axel smiled at her that afternoon she did not return his glance. The ship had shortened sail and rolled heavily on a cross-swell running from the west where Boston lay. There were few passengers on deck. Kate waited until Axel was occupied. She moved stealthily towards the doorway which led to his quarters. She brushed her hands against her skirt, cleaning them in preparation for the food she planned to steal. She was in his cabin, the box of biscuits in her hands, when he appeared quietly at the doorway.

"Ah! A visitor!" He seemed pleased to see her as he stepped through the narrow hatchway. "A hungry visitor!" He smiled broadly, taking the box from her hands and replacing it on the floor.

"Do you know the penalty for stealing at sea?" he asked.

Kate shook her head, too afraid to speak. His expression changed suddenly. "You'll be flogged, girl. Flogged with a leather whip." Then his voice softened again and his face grew less threatening. "If you wanted food you should have asked me. I'd have given you whatever you wanted, Kate. I'm your friend, you know that."

Kate drew away from him until her back was pressed against the porthole.

"I wanted it for my brother," she said. "He'll die unless he gets food today."

Axel nodded. "Yes. Your brother will die, and you'll be flogged." He paused, rubbing his hand across his mouth as if he was searching for a solution to the girl's problem. "There is a way," he said at last. "I have a way. Liam can have as much food as he can eat and so can you, and you needn't be flogged either."

"What do you mean?" Kate's fear showed. She trembled, her throat was dry.

"You know what I mean." Axel's voice was hard. There was no sign of friendship on his face. "Let's start with a kiss, shall we?" he said. "Or will I tell the captain we've a thief on board?"

"Don't flog me," Kate whispered. "Don't hurt me."

"Take what you want," Axel said. She took

what she knew she could wrap in the folds of her skirt.

"Put it on the ledge." He indicated a shelf beneath the porthole.

"Please close the curtain," Kate asked.

Axel pushed her on to the dirty bunk. He removed his belt and began to paw at her clothes.

Chapter Twenty-One

As the pain subsided and humiliation overwhelmed her, unbeknown to Kate the *Juno's* course closed with that of a vessel which had passed the same way eighteen months earlier. The *Devon Star* was a bigger, faster ship than that on which Kate and Liam had embarked, but like the *Juno* she also carried a cargo of Irish, although her passengers had been taken on in Liverpool. Like the *Juno*, she too was bound for Boston and among the three hundred on board was the young man from Lough Inagh of whom Kate O'Malley dreamed every night.

Tom Lynch still believed that he had murdered in Ireland, and in England he had stolen the money for his fare to Boston. He was in trouble in both countries, sought by pursuers he imagined behind him everywhere. But after his flight from Limerick to Liverpool, and once embarked in that great English port for Boston, his fears receded with each day that passed.

There was plenty of food on board the *Devon Star*, as well as water, and in three weeks she carried him swiftly across the north Atlantic, away from those who hunted him. He was free, he congratulated himself, he was well, he was no longer hungry. And no plague had struck his ship.

In 1845 the fever was not as widespread as it would become later and in those early months of the famine most of the passengers arriving in America did so hungry but in fair health. The *Devon Star* was well-provisioned and sound. For the most part her passengers were not discontent and her captain expected to make landfall in time for Christmas.

Tom Lynch had never doubted where he was heading. Boston was his ship's destination and it was in Boston that he planned to wait. But the *Devon Star* had departed late in the season, in early December, and towards the end of her journey one of the storms which howled down from Newfoundland each winter had caught up with her. Two mainsails had been blown out, spars had snapped and steerage had been lost. For almost three days the vessel yawed out of control, driven by a fearsome gale many miles south of her course, below Cape Cod and on towards Long Island from whose foot could be seen the city of New York.

Tom's heart sank as his hopes of landing in Boston grew more and more faint, but most of his fellow passengers cared less about where they landed then whether they landed at all. They were happy to make for the nearest port their captain could find and if that meant New York rather than Boston, then New York it would be. So, driven by the tail of the storm they went on, south and west, until the mighty city lay before their bow with its long wharves and its towering buildings and its immigration officers. The only remaining obstacle for Tom to overcome was to be admitted into America and as disembarkation grew closer all his old anxieties surfaced again. He remembered his attack on the policemen, the heavy blow to Blackstaff's head, the swift robbery of the shop in Liverpool. He had much to answer for. There was much to be afraid of.

"Name?"

"Fitzgerald."

"First name?"

"Niall."

"Where are you from?"

"County Limerick."

"Any family?"

"None still alive."

"Go on."

The line shuffled forward, almost imperceptibly. The air was arctic cold. Tom

Lynch stamped his feet to warm himself. Children cried from hunger and the weariness of standing.

"Name?"

"O'Driscoll."

"First name?"

"James."

"Where are you from?"

"County Cork."

"Any family?"

"I've a wife and two children left."

"Go on."

Tom was only three places from the front of the queue. His hands were damp with sweat. He imagined his interviewer's eyes on him, on Tom Lynch, murderer, thief. The man had a bundle of papers on the desk in front of him. A list of names surely, perhaps with a mark against the name of anyone wanted by the Irish or English police.

"Name?"

"Larkin."

"First name?"

"Úna."

"Where are you from?"

"Wicklow town."

"Family?"

"All dead."

"Go on."

But if I gave a false name here what might happen? Tom asked himself. If they have a list of passengers and I try another name, will they let me in?

Ahead of him a woman with three children was allowed through. Only one couple remained before it was his turn.

"Name?"

"O'Riordan."

"First name?"

"Seamus."

"Where are you from?"

"County Westmeath."

"Any family?"

"Only my wife."

"Go on then."

Tom was at the head of the queue. He had nothing which his hands could grip so he clasped his fingers behind his back. He could not feel shame at his past. He wanted to shout about it, to arrive as a hero, to tell the whole of America what Blackstaff had done, and Sir George Gerard; that Lough Inagh was no longer a place where people lived, that his life and his family had been destroyed and that he had been forced to flee.

"Name?"

"Lynch!"

The immigration officer looked up, surprised at the strength of the young man's voice.

155

"First name?"

"Tom! Tom Lynch!"

"Where are you from?"

"County Galway."

"Any family?"

"I'm alone."

The officer showed no more interest in Tom than he had in any of the others. There were three or four hundred of the wretches lined up inside the building and more outside. At anchor were several more ships waiting to disgorge their passengers. He would be at his desk until late in the afternoon. "Go on," he said to the young man. His eyes did not rise from the papers in front of him.

So Tom Lynch reached New York, setting foot on American soil in January 1846 with no knowledge of the city and not a friend to guide him. With a couple of other young men from the *Devon Star* he made for the teeming streets of Manhattan and then on, to the slums which formed the northern boundary of the city.

His step was less eager than he had expected, his heart less light than he had hoped, but at last he was free. He no longer needed to hide, he could begin to dream of a future, of Kate O'Malley and her brother who he knew would not be long in following him across the ocean.

Chapter Twenty-Two

For several days the *Juno* beat up and down the coast of Massachusetts across the westerly gale, but when dawn broke on the fourth day those passengers with the strength to reach the upper deck could see the coast clearly. Not the green, lush coast of their dreams, but a bleak, hard shoreline so swathed in mournful clouds and so completely lacking in colour that it could have been the coast of some barren northern fjord or an island of rock on which no man would ever wish to set foot.

The sun lifted the clouds as the day drew on and soon the land was revealed in a pattern of fields and woods, dotted here and there by small settlements of bright houses from which churches raised their shingled spires to a sky as blue as anyone on the *Juno* had ever known.

Finally, when land could be seen behind them as well as to their north and south, Boston itself appeared, a grey metropolis of stone and granite towers crowding down to the water's edge and stretching away almost as far as the eye could see. It filled valleys, climbed hills and crossed rivers and streams. It spread everywhere along the shoreline, absorbing whole towns which had once stood isolated, encroaching on grand estates where fine houses stood in acres of gardens and enveloping seaside villages where pleasure boats bobbed at their moorings.

To the passengers on board the *Juno*, shy country people who had come without exception from the hamlets and wiry valleys of Connemara, it was an unimaginable sight, as terrifying to them as might have been the loneliness of their lives to the inhabitants of the crowded streets of Boston. But they had to overcome their fears. Their destination lay before their eyes at last and they forced themselves to cheer with as much enthusiasm as if they had been shown the door to heaven itself.

By early evening they were at anchor in the harbour, some hundreds of yards from the busy quays, but safe and calm in the gentle swell of the hectic bay. A small boat had come alongside them on their arrival and a pair of officious men had peered over the rails. A doctor would be sent out the following day they said, to carry out a thorough inspection. In the meantime no one was to be allowed on or off the vessel. A barrel of fresh water was hoisted on board and the boat departed. The *Juno* was once more alone.

The wind died with the sunset and a half moon rose above the rigging of what seemed to Kate to be no fewer than a hundred ships. The noises of the city echoed across the water to where the *Juno* lay, her remaining complement of passengers at ease at last after so long at sea, but all of them in grief too. Hardly one among them had not lost a parent, a child or a sibling and for some, the horror was not yet over. For Kate it seemed as if the journey had been in vain. Some of the food she had got from Axel remained uneaten, while Liam lay semiconscious by her side. There was nothing more she could do but hold to his lips one of the biscuits she had accepted from the hideous man who had made her pay so dearly for them.

Every now and then she held her breath in order to listen to her brother's heart and several times she found herself weeping in frustration as she heard nothing but the sound of waves lapping the sides of the boat. By midnight, when the bells of the city rang with a confidence which was almost deafening, she had given up all hope. Liam lay like a ghost, his hands folded neatly across his chest as if he was already dead, his gaze blocked by eyelids which betrayed the fragile life they concealed by fluttering from time to time like the feeble wings of a young bird.

But by some miracle, or perhaps buoyed by the proximity of Boston, Liam survived the night, and the following morning he was able to sit on the upper deck, stronger than he had been for days, asking for water and more biscuit.

Oblivious to the means by which his sister had obtained the food, Liam chewed hungrily on everything she put before him and when she held a mug of water to his cracked lips, he gulped his fill of that too, and grinned at her. "I can see Boston," he assured her, again and again as he huddled beside her. "I didn't think I would ever make it. And I have you to thank for that, haven't I? It was you who saved me. God bless you, Kate."

"We're both here, Liam. That's all that matters. You have no need to thank me." Kate could hardly bear to return his trusting gaze.

"Do you think Tom will be here?" Liam was nervous with excitement at the thought of meeting his friend again. "He left long before us. He must be here by now, if it was to Boston he came, that is." He stopped himself and turned to Kate for reassurance. "He wouldn't have gone anywhere else would he? It was in Boston that we said we would meet?"

"I won't be wasting my time looking for Tom

Lynch," Kate told him. "He could be anywhere. Philadelphia or New York or Chicago. He could even be in California!" She spoke as if she was familiar with all the cities of the huge land she called Americkey, but she turned her head from her brother as she spoke and for a while her lips were set in a hard line which helped her suppress the tears she longed to shed.

"But don't you want to see Tom again?" Liam asked. "I thought he was the reason we came all this way. To Boston I mean. I thought you . . ."

"Hold your mouth, Liam O'Malley!" his sister ordered. "I'll have no time for Tom Lynch even if he is in Boston and he'll have no time for me, I'm sure." She kept her back to her brother as she spoke and Liam was too weak to move to face her.

"What are you saying?" he protested. "Tom's mad about you. He told me he'd never marry anyone else until he knew you were dead." Liam coughed and paused for a while to regain his breath, but Kate said not a word. "So don't go telling me that Tom Lynch won't want to see you if he's in Boston. He'll have plenty of time for you."

From the corner of her eye Kate could see Axel leaning against the rail a few paces from where she stood. "Everything's changed, Liam," she said. "We're in Boston now. Nothing will be the same here. I've forgotten Tom already. So don't go blathering on about him, d'ye hear?"

Their conversation petered out into a silence which left them both uncomfortable. Presently a small boat arrived at the *Juno*'s side and, with the crowd of passengers and crew all eager to hear the news, they forgot for the moment about Tom Lynch.

The captain stepped forward with Axel at his side to welcome the dapper man in a white suit who they all knew to be the doctor. But no one was able to overhear the conversation. Without delay the medic was ushered away to the captain's cabin and there the fate of the *Juno* was decided.

It took less than two minutes.

The dapper doctor almost ran from the captain's farewell, vaulting neatly over the rail and on to the bow of the cutter in which he had arrived. The captain stood, grim-faced, with his back to the open door of the passageway. The passengers crowded before him, their faces full of expectation. Some had packed their belongings in bundles, ready to disembark. Others, those who were still tending their sick relations, were less willing to ready themselves, unsure of how to cope with their new lives and how to deal with those dependent on them, now more than ever in the strange city which lay at their feet.

The captain leant across to Axel and whispered in his ear but when the Dutchman began to speak his words were of comfort to no one. "Doctor Adams has brought bad news," he began. "A ban has been imposed on all ships coming into Boston. The port is closed. No vessel is permitted to dock if there is a sign of illness aboard."

"Illness!" some of the passengers exclaimed as if the *Juno* was as clean as a convent. Others looked around at each other more honestly, assessing the chances of concealing their sores even from a blind man. "What sort of illness?" someone cried out.

"Your sort of illness." Axel did not bother to soften the blow of his words. "Typhus! Famine fever you call it! What most of you have! What the rest of you died from!" He flung his cap from his head in a gesture of frustration. "So we'll not be berthing in Boston! Not unless we stay here at anchor for three months without a death on board, and by the look of you lot and the amount of food you have left that doesn't seem too likely."

"What about New York?" a man called. Others took up the cry. "New York!" they yelled. "Why can't we go to New York?"

"New York is closed too!" Axel silenced their optimism with a raised hand. "There's only one place on this side of the Atlantic we can set you down and that's in Canada!"

"Canada? Canada?" The pathetic rag-clothed passengers took up the cry with almost no idea where it was, this unknown place where they would be able to leave their stinking ship.

"Can we go now to Canada?" called the man who a few seconds earlier had wanted to go to New York. "How long will it take? Is it far away?"

"It will take two weeks if all goes well," Axel shouted above the din of questions, "and tomorrow we can get supplies of fresh water. We'll set off in two days' time."

"What about food?" the women shouted. "We've nothing left at all. Anything we had kept back went this morning when we thought we would be getting off here."

"The British Consul will give us some money for food and the captain has offered to put in some cash of his own. We'll buy what we can and there's plenty of fish if you can bother yourselves to catch them," Axel said. "We can do no more. Food is your own responsibility. But we will be able to take on more fresh water tomorrow. That's the best we can do." He glanced at Kate, who stood against the ship's rail some way from the other passengers. He walked towards her but she turned her back to him. "Do you want more biscuit," he asked under his breath, "or anything else?" Kate felt his breath hot against the back of her neck. She ignored him and eventually he turned away to follow the captain. Kate's eyes were shut fast and she was shaking.

The last she heard of him was the tapping of his wooden soles on the planks of the sea-deck.

Chapter Twenty-Three

There were times during his first months in New York when Tom Lynch would willingly have returned to Galway to confront his fate, or even died. The cold was more intense than he could bear, the strangeness of the city alarmed him and loneliness sapped his energy. It was not that the immigrants from Ireland were unfriendly, but the people from the small settlements of the west were not used to strangers. For the most part they had remained in their quiet valleys with little contact with others. More often than not they married a near neighbour and they remained close to their families. Before the famine there had been neither reason nor opportunity to move and few people wanted to give up the warmth of those with whom they had grown familiar from childhood.

To Tom Lynch and those like him the cities of America were as fantastic as China or some distant planet. They knew no one and there was little of the warm-hearted hospitality to which they were accustomed. Loneliness became Tom's daily companion and dreaming was his only escape.

He found work soon enough, for he was young and strong, and there were not many men willing to spend their days loading sacks of coal and emptying them into the basements of the houses which surrounded the parks and avenues of the town centre. He could have the job until the warm weather came, some time in May, his employer had told him. During the summer there would be nothing for him, but if he wanted to come back in the autumn there might be more work. Tom accepted what was offered and made his plans.

In May or June, he told himself, he would go to Boston. It would take Kate and Liam that long to get there once the sailing season had begun and besides, if he worked the whole winter he might be able to save sixty or seventy dollars, enough for some decent clothes and a bit more besides. Then he would be able to face Kate and Liam with his head high. Then they could plan their futures together, the three of them.

He had grown in the months since his flight from the valley. He was taller and broader and with the long hours of bending and lifting each day his body had put on muscle where it had been slender and wiry. He shared a room with four others, two of them friends he had made on the *Devon Star*, and for immigrants they lived well enough. Tom saved what money he could. His only extravagance was to go each Saturday night to a smoky, low-ceilinged bar on the edge of Harlem where home-made whiskey could be bought for two cents a glass and not a word was spoken except in Irish.

In this uncomfortable shebeen he could forget the emptiness he felt whenever Kate's face appeared before him. It was there that he could listen to his friends congratulating themselves on the progress they were making in the strange city. It was there that he could pretend the smoking stove was a reminder of the fires his mother had lit in their cottage and only there that he could laugh and cry freely. And it was there on a spring night, when the lovely trees of Central Park were putting out bud, that Billy Garrett first found him; Garrett who had tracked him from Galway to Limerick, from Limerick to Liverpool and from Liverpool to New York. Garrett who carried with him always the Notice of Reward from Sir George Gerard, of two hundred pounds for information as to the whereabouts of Thomas Lynch, formerly of Lough Inagh, County Galway.

Not that Tom had noticed Blackstaff's right-hand man that first time, but Garrett had seen him. The brute who had put the torch to Tom's neighbours' home had stayed just long enough to be certain he had found his quarry, then he had slipped out into the street to prepare his attack. He knew Tom Lynch, he had seen him fight before. He knew he would not be easy to take.

It was more than a mile from the shebeen to the tenement building where Tom shared a room with his friends. The dark sky was patched with cloud and no one noticed the figure watching from the shadows as the young men left that night. No one turned to catch a glimpse of the heavy-footed shape which followed them as they sang their way home. No one noticed the grim face which leered outside their door as they climbed the stairs to their sleeping-place. But Garrett had marked his man. He would return with the villains he needed to help him. Tom Lynch's days in New York were numbered.

Chapter Twenty-Four

It took twelve painstaking days for the *Juno* to reach her final destination, a broad sweep of the mighty river Saint Lawrence a few leagues east of Quebec. Here, with every ship coming upriver required to lay up for inspection, almost two hundred vessels lay at anchor along the line of a wide bay formed by an arc in the river. They drifted on the current, sails furled and flags flying to indicate whether it was for food or water they waited, or an inspection by the medical officers who guarded this nautical gateway to Canada.

Ahead of the *Juno* lay a stretch of land which the captain had told them was called Grosse Isle, a long, heavily wooded island whose importance drew all the passengers on deck again. In spite of his excitement Liam could not summon the strength to stand and he clung to his sister's hand as she described what she saw.

"It's a big place," she began. There was

enthusiasm in her voice. "Much bigger than the islands on Lough Inagh, with the river flowing past on both sides. It's covered in trees too, beautiful tall trees, taller than I ever saw at home. I can see a village among the trees, with small low houses and the sunshine lighting them. There's a white church too, higher up, with grass and flowers all around it. Oh, Liam, we could be happy in Canada! You couldn't help but get well in a place like this." She was almost crying with relief and her brother's smile grew more and more serene with every word she used to describe the scene. Finally he clutched at her knees in order to drag himself to his feet and together they gazed at the island, enraptured by the tranquillity it suggested.

Among the houses Kate could see figures moving to and fro, flags flew from some of the larger buildings and an air of quiet activity seemed to occupy the place. It was a scene which anyone unfamiliar with the business of Grosse Isle might have thought idyllic. But the placid atmosphere of the island hid the truth: for many of those who arrived were never to leave.

As soon as it was possible each of the ships moored below Grosse Isle was visited by one or other of the doctors who worked on the island. For most of the vessels the inspection was a matter of routine and they were free to weigh anchor and be on their way without delay as soon as the medical officers had completed their task. But for those from Ireland, the Coffin Ships, as they had come to be known, the inspection was merely the beginning. There was not a ship among them allowed to continue on up the river. One by one, as their filthy condition and the extent of the fever they carried were discovered, they were ordered to sail on for a short distance, to lie in the lee of Grosse Isle and disembark their festering cargo of the gaunt and the near dead on to the tiny emerald island which for many would become their grave.

But at first, for the young travellers from Lough Inagh, it was almost as if they had arrived in heaven. Liam struggled to the deck and clung to the rail as they tacked tediously upriver and eventually dropped anchor so close to the shore of the island that they could smell the trees and grass and earth which would soon be theirs. The summer sun shone on their necks and heads and even the waters of the river seemed to come to life, as blue as the deepest sea under a cloudless sky.

There was a long delay before disembarkation could commence and the passengers' enthusiasm for the island waned at the sight before them. Despite its beauty, Grosse Isle, they saw, was an island of death. A fleet of little boats threaded their way through the waiting ships, laden with corpses, their cargoes lying in haphazard piles, scarcely disguised by crude wrappings and so numerous that after an hour or so none of the onlookers bothered to count them. It seemed to Kate like a scene from hell, and she shivered with fear at the thought that her dear brother had come so close to being one among the countless bodies being taken away. But Liam had survived, she had saved him and they were together. The encounter with Axel was behind her. There was food at last and soon they would be gone, away from the *Juno*, away from the man who had shamed her.

When their turn came they were permitted to disembark. A tender pulled alongside, then another, and without delay the twenty or so surviving passengers were taken off. But the men handling the small boats would not touch the sickly Irish and those too weak to climb down the rope ladders had to submit to manhandling by their friends or families while the oarsmen looked on, or more frequently, averted their gaze, nauseated by the filthy condition of their charges.

It took less than half an hour to empty the *Juno* of its cargo and then, beneath a hot, mid-summer sun, Kate and Liam stood on the fresh grass of Grosse Isle with their fellow passengers,

173

some with what remained of their possessions hanging from their hands, others with nothing in the world but the rags they wore.

Two doctors and a collection of religious workers eyed them uneasily. Some among the passengers were too ill to stand. One, a lank-haired child of three or four, was dying in her father's arms, her tiny frame heaving as she gasped for breath. The remainder, numb with fear and exhausted from the weeks of starvation, were listless. The excitement of their arrival had passed, to be replaced by disappointment. They were still hungry; the sores which had festered for weeks on their bodies had not vanished; the weariness which had dragged at them still weighed them down.

Liam sat beside his sister, as gaunt as a piece of driftwood and, in the bright daylight Kate noticed for the first time the transparency of his skin and the tightness of his lips, stretched in a permanent smile across his teeth. He shivered too, although the air was warmer than any he had experienced in Ireland, and he wrapped his arms around himself like a child warding off an assailant.

The doctors wanted to separate them, but Kate would have none of it and Liam clung to her so fiercely that they were shown instead to a tent where families could stay together. They were taken to a central kitchen where food was prepared and they were encouraged to drink water, but those supervising the distribution gave them little enough to eat, Kate noticed, and slowly, in order that their bodies could retain the unaccustomed food.

After they had eaten they talked. Liam was full of praise and gratitude for his sister and he spoke of how he would repay her when his health returned. He had guessed nothing of the means she had employed to obtain food on board the *Juno* and Kate would not speak of those dark days. Even to hear him discussing the miracle of his survival was more than she could bear and when he went on to start planning the remainder of their journey, out of Canada and on to Boston, she could not respond. She put her hand over his mouth to silence him.

"We must send a letter home, Liam," she said. "There'll be someone here who could write in Irish for us and we'll send it to the poorhouse, just to tell Mammy we've arrived and we're alive."

Liam nodded agreement. "Yes," he said, and he began to cough again, "I suppose we're alive." He thought for a while before speaking again. "Perhaps Axel would take something for us. I heard him saying they would be going back to Galway."

The thought of home made him want to talk and he spoke of Tom Lynch and what they would do when they met up again. Perhaps they could work together, he suggested. Perhaps Tom and Kate would "make a go of it", he said.

"No," she whispered. "No, Liam." She turned to face him, taking his hands in hers as one might to comfort a child. "Too much has happened. Everything has changed, Liam. I'm not the same person any more. I don't want to talk about it, not Tom and me together. That can't happen. It's over."

"But I wanted it too, Kate." Tears sprang from her brother's eyes. "I've thought about it so often. You and Tom, my two best friends, together. We would have been like a family again, even here, so far from home. Remember that day sitting on the rock above the lake, how we talked about it, the three of us." He rubbed his thin forearm along his eyes. "We're so alone here, and Tom must be too. He'll be missing us, don't you think?

Kate turned her face from his, tears of remorse and despair coursing down her cheeks. She could hardly imagine the pain of setting eyes on Tom again. She could never tell him what had happened on the journey, and equally she could not marry him unless he knew everything about her. She must put him out of her mind and at all costs she must avoid meeting him.

She stood and smoothed the folds of her skirt. "I need to be alone for a time," she said. "I need to walk, to be beside the water." She bent to kiss her brother on the cheek and strode swiftly away.

Later that day, when she had climbed to the highest point on the island and lain for a while in the sun, she enquired in the hospital and found a woman, an emigrant like herself, but from Galway town. The woman had been to school and she was more than willing to write a letter for the girl from Lough Inagh. Kate found herself almost devoid of words when it came to describing their journey, but the letter was short, and soon it was finished. She sealed it as best she could and took it back to her brother. Liam persuaded an oarsman from one of the small boats to deliver it to Axel and they watched as the man set off towards the *Juno* where she lay at anchor not far from the jetty. The sun was behind him, outlining him with its glare and making prisms of each droplet of water as he dipped and raised the oars into the river. "God bless you!" Liam called as the tiny vessel moved away.

At nightfall mosquitoes and other insects emerged which tormented them and attacked the sores on their exposed limbs as they tossed and turned. Kate could not sleep. Nothing had turned out as they had planned, but still she persuaded herself that she could be happy. She had survived; and here, she thought, in this near perfect place she would rebuild her strength. She reached out to rest her hand on Liam as he slept beside her, his breathing measured and peaceful for the first time in weeks.

For a long time she lay awake, but eventually, lulled by the quiet gliding of the river past its banks, she fell into unconsciousness, disturbed only by a vision of Tom Lynch, as clear as if he was close enough to hold her, as warm as he had been in the bracken at Ballyconneely with apples and plums in his pockets and his hand outstretched to her in the darkness. Against her will she felt herself submitting to the dream, felt her hands wanting to respond to his touch and her face smiling with happiness at his arrival by her side. But then she woke and sat upright, once more overwhelmed by anger and self-hatred. She told herself again that she could not allow such thoughts, that Tom Lynch could never be part of her life, that she had disgraced his love for her and hers for him, that she must avoid him, must never let him find her. She would go through life, she told herself, smeared with the stain of her sin with Axel.

At that the face of the little Dutchman rose before her, his mouth open, his smile coarse and knowing. His arms stretched out to her, his hands felt for her, his stubby fingers grasped her wrists and then she was fully awake again, sweating and gasping for breath.

Liam coughed harshly, the noise wrenching her from the nightmare. As she turned to him he doubled up and a series of longer, deeper sounds racked his chest and throat. Kate looked down at him, trying to distract herself from her fears by the mere fact of her brother's continued existence. As she watched she noticed a trickle of half-digested food gurgling almost imperceptibly from his mouth followed by a stream of something darker, smoother, more ominous.

She reached out to her brother's face, already fearing what she would find, but even so the warmth of the blood spilling on to his jaw surprised her and she drew her hand away quickly. Liam began coughing again, but this time with less strength and she sensed it was the end.

Chapter Twenty-Five

The nuns and nurses wrapped his body in canvas, that being all there was, and the stiff corpse, so meagre that it might have been the body of a child, was carried on to a small boat in which several others had already been dumped.

Kate could no longer cry. Desolation overwhelmed her, settling on her face like a mask, narrowing her eyes and forcing her mouth into a shape so tight and rigid that her teeth ached. An elderly Frenchman with a long moustache offered to take her arm as she climbed into the boat but she ignored the gesture and the wooden seat to which he tried to direct her, kneeling instead astride the centre thwart with her hands resting lightly on the shoulders of her dead brother.

The rowers pulled at their oars and the vessel moved off slowly across the glassy river. At the far end of the island a promontory of land had been set aside as a burial-ground. Even from a distance Kate could see that it swarmed with people. A few of them were mourners, tragic, still figures, perhaps like her the sole survivors of their families. The others, local men mainly, had been pressed into service by authorities unable to cope with the sheer numbers of the dead.

All the while more corpses arrived until, after an hour or so, Kate no longer thought of them as the bodies of humans, of men, women and children. To have accepted them as people, like herself and her brother, was beyond her imagination. They were sacks of meal or grain, she began to believe, or bundles of straw and reeds. They had never been living beings, could not possibly have been, not in such numbers, and as the long canvas parcels were placed side by side in a communal grave she found herself unable even to pray. She stood motionless, guilty to be still alive and wishing with all her strength that her heart would stop its incessant beating and leave her free to die.

When the pit was full the workmen took up their spades. Kate closed her eyes and listened to the thud as each clump of earth was tossed on to the bodies in the pit.

Finally, while the sun at her back lit in vivid green the trees and grass of the island and warmed the skin of her neck, the workmen paused in their efforts and she opened her eyes.

A layer of earth lightly covered the bodies and stones were being added to weigh them down. Under the mantle of soil which covered the corpses she could still make out the shape of Liam's frame close to the edge of the pit. She walked towards it, surprised that her eyes were dry and, taking a flat river stone from a pile beside her, she knelt, raised it to her lips and kissed it before laying it where she thought her brother's heart would be. Then she got to her feet and walked away.

The Frenchman took her arm to guide her back to the boat and this time she allowed him to help. She stumbled aboard and seated herself, aware that the old man wanted merely to offer sympathy, but unwilling to release her anguish by acknowledging him.

She looked around her. The line of funeral boats continued to arrive at the burial-ground; the unloading continued; the lifting of the bodies continued; the laying in the pits continued; the scattering of earth continued; the weighing down of the bodies continued; and then each boat turned from the shore, lighter in the water, to set off for a new cargo. The circle was complete and the supply of bodies never-ending, enormous, unimaginable. Did we leave Ireland for this? Kate asked herself. Is this the new life we have won? She clenched her hands until the nails of her fingers drew blood from her palms and she closed her eyes as tightly as she could.

Years later, when these events could be contemplated without grief, people reckoned that in that one frightful year more than twenty thousand bodies had been laid to rest on Grosse Isle, men, women and children, and all of them Irish. Yet for Kate O'Malley that day there was only one body which mattered. Liam had gone. She was alone in the world.

The little boat rocked in the swell of a large vessel making its way down river. The oarsmen checked their stroke and Kate, turning her gaze at last from the fading burial-ground, felt herself overwhelmed with nausea. She leant her head over the gunwale and was surprised to find herself retching violently into the water.

Chapter Twenty-Six

Axel opened Kate's letter a few hours after the *Juno* had weighed anchor. The old ship, reeking from the lime which had been used to disinfect her hold, slipped easily down the river, pushed by the eager current and a fresh westerly wind. The *Juno* was going back to Galway.

"Dear Mammy," the Dutchman read,

"*Liam and I are in Canada, on Grosse Isle which is near Quebec, so we haven't made it to Boston yet. The journey was not good. The water barrels burst and there was not enough food on the boat. A lot of people died. Liam was pretty bad but we're still alive, thank God.*

We didn't care much for the crew, one of them treated me very badly, but we're away from them now and it's beautiful here.

We will write again soon with better news.

Your loving daughter,

Kate."

The little Dutchman scowled as he read. "Treated her bad, did I?" he muttered to himself. "Well, we don't want that getting back to Galway." He screwed the letter up into a crisp ball and raised it in his hand as if to toss it into the river, but at the last minute he changed his mind, unravelled the crinkled paper and proceeded to tear it into small pieces which he dropped into the deep, swirling waters of the *Juno's* wake.

Chapter Twenty-Seven

It was late April in New York and the day had been warm when they came looking for Tom Lynch. Garrett himself remained outside with his men. One of them slipped quietly into the building. The flimsy shutters which in winter kept the shebeen cosy had been thrown open and the door was ajar, letting light into the room. The man stood to one side as he searched the faces of the crowd. It was not by chance that Tom looked up – he had noticed the intruder at once. His clothes were not those of the usual customers. He had not been seen there before.

The stranger made his way towards the unlit stove, rattling a few heavy coins in his pocket. He stopped and spoke to a drinker, someone unknown to Tom, who shook his head. The man moved on, the coins now visible in his hand. He asked another, closer to Tom. This time his words could be heard. "I'm looking for Tom Lynch," said the stranger, "a young fella. Drinks here sometimes I'm told." He looked about himself as if to show familiarity with the surroundings. "I'm a friend of his. From Connemara." The second drinker shook his head and the stranger moved closer.

Tom turned to face the man. "I know where to find Tom Lynch," he said. "Who's looking for him?"

"Mallon's the name." The stranger held out his hand. "Where can I find him?"

"He's here in this room," Tom said. He smiled. "If you're his friend you should be able to recognise him."

"It's been a long time." Garrett's man looked around himself sheepishly. "It's a while since I saw him. He was just a boy then. Point him out to me will you?"

"What do you want him for?" Tom was wary now. This was no friend, he knew. He had never seen the man before.

"Let's talk outside," said the stranger. "There's money here for the right information."

Tom's eyes scanned the room. His friends were close by, but still, there was only one door, only one way out. "Tom Lynch can't be bought with that," he said, nodding at the silver dollar in the man's hand. But the stranger's insistence was threatening. Tom was worried, his anger was rising. "Get out now with your money and your lies!" He spoke loudly. "You never knew Tom Lynch in your life!"

The man shook his head and scowled. "It was only to do him a favour that I was looking for him." He slipped the coin into his pocket and turned on his heel. "But don't worry," he called over his shoulder. "I'll find him. I'm getting close to him now. I know that."

Tom waited a few minutes. His friends had overheard the exchange of words. They told him to stay, not to worry. They would all go home together, they agreed, even though the fellow had been on his own. There was no danger, they declared, no cause for concern.

But Tom knew otherwise. Only Tom knew that there was a reward on his head, that he might be thrown out of America or into jail if the police in New York heard of his past. Someone was on to him. He had to go. He had to leave as soon as possible.

He bade his friends farewell and walked from the drinking house. The street was lit by moonlight. Ahead of him a feeble lamp guttered. There were few passers-by and no traffic. The silence was eerie. He was only a few steps from the door of the shebeen when they came at him.

They attacked from behind, two of them, and pinioned his arms before he had even heard them. A third stepped out from the darkness. A knife-blade shone. A fourth held a truncheon of some sort, thwacking it against the palm of his hand. Tom struggled, but he was powerless and

188

outnumbered and the knife flickered an inch or two from his throat. He held himself quite still.

When Garrett made his appearance it was some time before Tom recognised him. The high shoulders and low brows of his pursuer were familiar, but he was shorter and more thickset then Tom remembered. His hands were jammed into his pockets. He wore a misshapen black hat with a broad brim, but when he tipped back his head the street lamp drew the shadows from his roughly shaven face, and Tom Lynch knew him.

"Got you at last, you Papist bastard," Garrett sneered. "Three months I spent lookin' for you in Boston," his voice was low and menacing, "before I figured out you must have landed somewhere else. But never mind. Here we are. I only wish Blackstaff could be here to see this." He aimed a kick at the young man's groin, but Tom was able to swing away from the blow and Garrett's boot glanced instead off his thigh. "Bastard!" he said again. "Three wasted months!" He aimed another boot at the young man, this time to better effect and Tom grunted with the pain.

Summoning all his strength Tom turned towards the door from which he had just emerged. He dragged air into his chest, opened his throat and let out a roar which could have been heard a block away. The man with the knife darted in front of him again, but Tom let fly with one foot and flattened him with a powerful kick.

The pair holding him felt their grip loosen and he bent double suddenly, heaving them over his back as a bear might shrug off a pair of hounds. Garrett took a step backwards, blocking the view of the man with the club, and from the door of the shebeen came the sounds of running feet as Tom's companions came to his aid.

Sensing the danger before any of his men, Garrett stepped further back, hiding himself in the gloom as punches were thrown and heads were kicked. It did not last long. Even the armed men were no match for the enraged Irishmen and Tom's attackers, surprised by the sudden arrival of his supporters, were soon sprawled about, moaning, nursing their injuries and cursing loudly.

Despite his disappearance Garrett had not got away. Tom had watched him and knew he was cornered. He followed him to an unlit doorway, stopping a few yards from him. The young man was breathing hard from the fight. He waited to recover his breath. When he spoke his voice was as hard and cold as gunmetal.

"I could kill you, Garrett, you know. I should kill you after what you've done to me. You and those thugs." He indicated the men groaning on the roadway. "What do you want anyway?"

"I want you, Lynch. That's what I've come here for. And I'll get you yet. There's a reward, you know, for what you did to Blackstaff and the two policemen whose heads you cracked open."

"Good!" Tom spat the word in his assailant's face. "If you had half a brain you'd know that we're even now! My family has been destroyed. How many of them are dead by now? How many others are starving, here or back home? Because of you and people like you! I should kill you now!" He looked behind him to where his friends stood. They said nothing, offered no advice. They knew nothing of his past nor of Garrett's reasons for pursuing him.

"Come away, Tom!" one of them called. "Whoever he is he's not worth it. Come on home!"

"I can't leave it like this!" the young man answered. "He can still harm me. He can still cause me trouble. I can't stay in New York if he's here." He shook his head in fury. "I have to go or I have to kill him!"

Chapter Twenty-Eight

So great was the number of Irish fleeing to North America in the autumn of 1847 that the period of quarantine on Grosse Isle had to be reduced from the usual forty days in order to accommodate the influx. Supplies of medicine were inadequate, there were not enough doctors and nurses, there was insufficient food. Four weeks after Liam had died Kate O'Malley was allowed to depart.

Her health had improved on Grosse Isle but she did not want to stay in one of the makeshift huts to which those without obvious symptoms of illness were sent. So bad had the overcrowding become that for those like her, well enough to survive, but destitute, the only space available was to be found in tents close to the hospital where she passed her period of quarantine among the emaciated beings who waited for death.

Four weeks had to pass during which she could prove her health while even the doctors and nurses, French-Canadians mostly, were succumbing to the cholera or typhus which raged throughout the hospital. And Kate was not at all sure of her health. Since her arrival on the island she had begun vomiting at regular intervals and she knew that her weak frame, starved after the weeks at sea, would be incapable of supporting her if she could not keep down some of the food now provided for her.

She did not fully understand her illness, yet something about it alarmed her. She recalled her mother retching just as she herself had begun to do, but for her mother there had been a reason which all the family understood, and they had talked openly of the child which was growing in her belly.

Kate took to walking alone whenever she could, meandering under the lovely trees which blanketed the gentle slopes of the island, or strolling on the grassy banks which stretched along its shores. At times she would sit on a rock or wade into one of the shallow bays where the river encroached on the land, allowing her feet to cool in the clear water and a patch of sand to blanket her toes as it had done so long ago on the beach in Connemara.

Sometimes she would talk of the future with the other immigrants. Like her, there were many people alone on the island, having lost every member of their families and without exception they had no idea what to do once they were free to go. After four or five weeks, if they showed no signs of the fever, they would be able to move on, to Quebec or Montreal, even as far as Toronto, and there they would start their new lives. But the immigrants from Ireland knew nothing of life in the vast land or the busy cities of Canada. They had no ambition except to survive.

They had set out originally for Boston, many of them, and they thought they would know Boston. Of Canada they were completely ignorant. They had no skills, no money and no friends. They knew nobody who could help them. And autumn was approaching. The days were shortening and the sun, even at its peak, no longer drove the pale-skinned Irish into the shade. When the breeze blew from the north, which it did from time to time, and the migrant birds departed and the black squirrels foraged across Grosse Isle for their winter hoards, the air seemed suddenly threatening and ominous.

By October, although Kate was still vomiting nearly every day, the doctors said she should leave the island. She showed no signs of fever and her skin, which had grown pale and almost opaque on board the *Juno*, seemed to have filled out a little and taken on some colour. Her eyes too were clearer and her hair, so long neglected, but washed now in the soft river water which surrounded the island, had regained its sheen and every day she teased it into the curls and waves she had almost forgotten she had.

Those leaving were asked where they wanted to go, about a hundred of them, lined up at the jetty which protruded into the bay from the small township which had grown up on the island. They had no idea whether they would be better off in Quebec or Montreal, they knew nothing of either city, but they had to make the choice. In Toronto, Kate knew, the people spoke English, and she knew a few words of English. Some of the French-Canadian nurses had tried to persuade her to go to Quebec or Montreal, but she knew no French so she asked to be taken to Toronto.

But there was no boat departing for Toronto that day, only a flat-bottomed tender bound for Montreal, so to Montreal she went. From there, she told herself, she would walk, not knowing that more than two hundred miles separated the two cities.

After the peace of Grosse Isle, Montreal was mayhem. The city was a confusing maze of streets, and so big that Kate, used to the quiet valley of her childhood, her only experience of cities being the little town of Galway, was overcome with fear. Nobody would speak to her although there were people everywhere, especially men, hard, violent men who fought and spat and shouted and paid no attention to the young Irish girl except to eye her as callously as they might a mare or a bullock offered for sale in a market.

There was nowhere for the immigrants to sleep and no work. Indeed, Kate had no idea how to go about finding work even if there had been any for her, so she joined the throngs of Irish on the streets, begging when they could and stealing when there was no one to beg from. They slept where they hoped the wind could not chill them, huddled together like domestic animals in a blizzard, in doorways or under bridges, wrapping themselves in whatever they could find, paper or sacking if they were lucky, or even holding tight to a stray dog if nothing else was to hand. A dog might pant and snore throughout the night, but a dog was warm, warm and alive.

And all the time the Canadian winter bore down on them. Soon the deaths began again, as the November snows fell, whitening the ledges and roofs of the buildings and stretching along the branches of the trees which stood bare in the parks and gardens. There was no respite from the cold. By December the city lay blanketed in winter, the residents came less often on to the streets, the traffic thinned and only the immigrants, the wretched poor from the hills and valleys of Ireland, were still to be seen, desperate in their need and wild with hunger.

Kate knew she must move on if she was to survive. Montreal could not feed her and her stomach craved food. She had intended to go to Toronto, she reminded herself, and in the company of another woman, Mary, a young mother from Mayo, widowed during the sea journey and childless after Grosse Isle, she set off in the last chill days of 1847.

They travelled on foot at first, but presently one of the covered wagons which plied their route caught up with them and the driver offered them a place. They clambered aboard gratefully and made almost forty miles in the day. The following morning they set off on foot again but soon another, smaller dray picked them up and they could save their energy once more. In this way they completed their journey, arriving in the English city in less than a week. They had even eaten on the route, thanks to the generosity of one of the wagon drivers, and they were full of hope as they stood by the shore of the great lake which seemed almost to surround the town.

But as soon as they headed into the streets where they knew they must find their means of survival they saw that their problems were not over. Toronto was little different from Montreal.

Gangs of beggars thronged every alley and besieged every large building, From their ragged clothes and bare feet Kate was in no doubt that the people she saw were Irish and while she pitied them their plight she could hardly bear to acknowledge their existence.

She turned away, tears of frustration in her eyes, and collapsed into the arms of her companion. "We can't stay here," she wept. "It's no better here than in Montreal."

"I can't go on the roads again," Mary replied. "I've had enough travelling. I need to stay here a while. I need to rest." They clutched each other for comfort. They scarcely knew each other but they had no one else to hold, and although Mary made no mention of it she knew, as a mother, that Kate too should rest, that the swelling at Kate's waist was not from an excess of food. She feared for her friend's well-being.

As they stood bewildered in the street a man came towards them. "Who are you with?" he demanded angrily in Irish. At least he is one of us, Kate thought, taking in his ragged condition, even if he is unfriendly. She tried to smile at him, but his scowl did not waver. "This is our territory! Who are you?"

"We've come from Montreal. We arrived today. What do you mean it's your 'territory'? We've a right to be here too."

"You can't beg here. That's what I'm saying. This is our street and if you want to stay you must join us. Otherwise we'll drive you out." He stood close to them now, his eyes glaring into theirs, his face pumping with rage. He was young, Kate saw. No more than twenty she thought. Too young to be so fierce.

"Well? What are you going to do? If you won't join us we'll move you on ourselves. If you stay you have to obey the rules and we'll share what we have. But no begging on your own. Understand?" He seemed to be softening towards them now and Kate sensed his embarrassment.

"We'll join with you," she told him and Mary nodded agreement. "I've begged in Galway and I've begged in Montreal," Kate went on, "so there's nothing you can teach me about begging, but I'll join you if it will make you happy."

The young man's scowl softened. "There's nothing left here anyway," he admitted, lowering his shoulders and allowing the anger to fall from his face. "I don't know why we stay. The locals despise us. The begging's useless now. Look!" He pointed at the crowd milling around a coach a few yards away. "One carriage and eighty or ninety people hoping to get a meal off it. It's hopeless. God knows what we're going to do here in a few days time. I'm not staying here to die.

I'm going to Boston. There's food there, and work too, I hear."

"Where do you sleep?" Kate asked.

"Where we can. Under a bridge if it's raining or snowing. In a hedge or beneath a bush if it's not." The young man smiled. "In Boston there are buildings where people like us can get a room, I'm told, with windows and doors and clean floors. I'm going to Boston!" His confidence in Boston seemed to grow as he described it to the two women and he nodded as if he was confirming something he already knew to be true. "Boston it is," he declared. "Boston's for me. And if there's nothing there for us we'll go on, further south, to New York or Philadelphia or Baltimore, where the sun shines so hot you can walk naked in the streets."

Kate was so bemused by the thought of streets full of people walking naked that she almost smiled, but she had never heard of Baltimore before and she was so intrigued by the extensive geographical knowledge of the young man who confronted her that she wanted to hear more.

"So how do you get to Baltimore?" she asked.

"Well, first you go to Boston," said the young man and then you go on, to New York and Phila . . ." His face filled with enthusiasm. He liked the look of Kate O'Malley and he wanted a companion.

"But if I don't want to go to Boston first," Kate interrupted. "What if I want to go straight to Baltimore?"

"You can't do that. You have to go first to Boston," the adventurer told them, although in truth he had no idea where Baltimore lay. "There's no other way." He grinned at the two women. "Let's go," he said. "Let's go tomorrow."

"But what about your friends?" asked Mary. She pointed to the crowd of beggars to which the young man had claimed to belong. "And why should we go? We've only just arrived. Maybe we should stay a while to try our luck here, in Toronto. . ." She could not bring herself to look at Kate's protruding belly, not in the presence of the young man, but she knew she must warn Kate against travelling again so soon.

The fellow shook his head and held out his hand. "Peadar FitzGibbon," he announced, "from County Clare. Will you travel with me?"

He had a fresh face and a smile which Kate felt she could trust. His feet were bare and his trousers hung in tatters just below his knees. The only part of his dress which gave any confidence was a fur jacket, many sizes too big for him, which swamped his narrow frame and curled up around his ears.

"I stole it if you must know," he said, in response to Kate's suspicious stare. "We steal everything here, we all do. There's no other way. I need some shoes though. I can't arrive in Boston without shoes can I? And nor can you." He looked at Kate's cloth-bound feet, wrapped in the remains of the woollen scarves given to her the day she had left Galway. "If I get you some boots will you come with me?"

"Stolen boots?"

"How else will I get them?"

Kate nodded. Stealing was hardly a grave sin, she thought, after what she had done on board the *Juno*, and her feet were sore and numb with cold. She was more concerned to find herself thinking of embarking on a journey with someone she had known for only a few minutes. She knew she should stay away from Boston, but at least, she told herself, it was a start. She did not want to remain in Toronto and perhaps, from what Peadar said, Baltimore would not be much further than Boston.

"Give me till dark. I'll meet you here," said the young man. "We'll start out tomorrow morning." Without waiting for a reply he set off at a trot towards the crowd of beggars. He stopped to talk to an older man, pointing back to Kate and Mary as if explaining something. The two women found themselves being examined from a distance. Eventually the older man seemed to nod agreement and Peadar waved confidently before walking on.

"We can stay," said Mary, "though why anyone should want to stay I don't know." She leant back against a wall and breathed a sigh of relief. Then she took Kate's hand nervously, wanting to talk. "We don't know much about each other, do we?" she began.

Kate nodded agreement.

"Were you ever married?" Mary asked.

Kate began to shake her head vigorously then thought better of it. "Well . . ." she began, "he . . . he . . . died . . . on the journey." Kate lied to conceal the shame of her pregnancy. Mary looked doubtful, but she changed the subject.

"Do you think you should be travelling?" the Mayo woman went on. "In that state." She lowered her eyes to the mound beneath the younger girl's waist.

"What d'you mean?" Kate would rather have talked of anything else.

"D'you not think you might be . . . that there might be a baby there?" Mary blurted out.

Kate could not meet her companion's steady gaze.

"You shouldn't be travelling you know, not if . . . if you're that way. You could lose the child, and hurt yourself."

"Yes," Kate said, as if she had no interest in the baby, or hardly believed it existed. The fear which had dogged her since she had first been sick on Grosse Isle now reared up before her and she was overcome with loneliness. This was something she did not know how to confront. Tears began to fill her eyes and to put a stop to the conversation she waved Mary from her and fixed her gaze on a distant building. After a while they walked a few steps together, but neither could think of a way of breaking the silence between them.

Scraps of bread were brought to them as the afternoon wore on and later a barrel of watery soup was carted in. In a few minutes the street was crowded with hundreds of beggars. There was not enough for everyone, desperate voices were raised, food was dropped and soup spilt. Soon the women delivering the sustenance had to withdraw and in the chaos fights broke out over the smallest of crusts. Kate could hardly believe her own countrymen and women could act in such a way. She herself got nothing.

Soon after dusk Peadar returned carrying a sack under his arm and sporting a pair of long brown riding-boots on his legs. The two women had hardly moved from the spot where he had left them. He squatted in front of them and opened the sack, taking from it a couple of men's shoes, one black and in poor condition, the other covered in mud and made of a soft material Kate had never seen before.

"Suede," Peadar announced as he proffered it to her, too shy to put it on her foot himself. "It's very warm," he added. Kate did not want to ask him where he had got the ill-matched footwear. He was proud of his afternoon's work and bursting with news of his plans for the next day. The black boot had a higher heel than the other and when Kate had them both on she found it difficult to walk, but immediately her feet began to warm and she thanked the young man gratefully.

"We have to cross the lake first," Peadar told the two women. "We need to head east," he explained, "and I've found just the thing for us. There's a load of timber going by ferry to Syracuse. That's in New York State," he added, "and a fellow I know is in charge of the shipment. He'll get us on board. It's a steamer too, so it will be quick."

Kate found herself warming to the young man. If she must travel with anyone to get out of Canada, she thought, it might as well be with someone who is good company, and besides, she told herself, there was no one else in her life, not a soul on the continent who even cared that she existed.

Mary had already announced her intention of remaining in Toronto. "I'm not going anywhere," she had said. "And you're in no state to travel

205

either," she had warned her friend. But Kate had hushed her with a scowl. She did not want Peadar to think of her as a burden and she was determined to go. She pleaded with Mary to accompany her but the Mayo woman was adamant. "I'll help you if you stay," she said. "And I'll look after you. Lord, didn't I have two little ones of my own when I left Ireland, so I know what to do. But I won't come with you, Kate, and you shouldn't go. Stay and let me help you."

So insistent was the young widow that Kate was torn. She wanted so badly to stop travelling, to rest for a time, to regain her strength. But there was no food in Toronto and every gust of wind from the north reminded her that the worst of the winter was still to come. She wanted to leave the other beggars behind her, to head south and, brave as she was, she did not want to travel alone into America.

When Peadar offered to go with her all the way to Baltimore she clung to Mary and thanked her, but she insisted she would not stay. Somehow, in the sunshine of the south, she hoped, life would not be so bad. There would be work of some sort, there must be farms near Baltimore and she was a good worker. Hadn't her father always told her she was as good as any of her brothers in a field of potatoes?

She needed to get her health back though. The vomiting seemed to have stopped, and for that she thanked God, but she still felt weak, still feared the existence of a baby beneath her tightening waist. She had cramps in her stomach most of the time too, from the hunger she supposed, and that was not going to go away quickly. There were no signs that there was more food in Canada than there had been on board the *Juno* and now she had to use so much energy walking. She longed for a day, just one day would be enough, during which she could sit and eat her fill and rest.

Chapter Twenty-Nine

Peadar woke her before dawn on a morning so bitter she could hardly hold her eyes open. They rose from their cold resting-place at the foot of a tree and stretched the stiffness from their joints. There was a fog across the lake and the surface of the water was so still and lifeless that at first they thought it must have frozen solid in the night. But as they approached the quayside a solitary duck trailed its wake into view and they sighed with relief knowing that the ferry would be able to sail.

They arrived too early and there was no sign of Peadar's friend, no sign of life at all. Even the ferry's engines were quiet. They loitered about on the quay until a group of other passengers arrived, rich people, Kate saw, with hats and clean shoes and warm coats, and leather luggage for their clothes, people who talked loudly, unafraid of drawing attention to themselves.

They heard the ferry's engines start up and felt the vibrations rumbling through the timbers of the wharf. Brown smoke billowed from the stack and swirled about the boat, its acrid smell reminding Kate faintly of the turf fires which had warmed her family's cottage on the shores of Lough Inagh, but this was a harsher smell and soon she found it irritating her nose, causing her to hold her breath until it passed and a patch of cleaner air came her way.

A youth appeared at the ferry's rail, leaning nonchalantly on one arm as he surveyed the crowd beginning to gather below him. Peadar nudged Kate, then turned his back to the boat until a short, shrill whistle pierced their ears. Suddenly Kate felt her arm taken in an urgent grip and she was walking, almost running up the gangway and on to the covered deck. They did not stop. The youth was ahead of them, beckoning them towards a passageway and further into a small cupboard in which brushes and buckets were stored, and lengths of rope and a motley collection of ship's goods. They lurched in and stumbled, rattling and crashing among the contents of their hiding-place.

They heard the door slammed shut behind them. Some sort of a bolt was rammed across it. They were in complete darkness. Not a word had been spoken, but they were safely on board.

"Who is he?" Kate asked, hardly able to see her companion in the gloom of their hideout.

"A lad from Ennis," Peadar whispered. "Not twenty miles from my own village. I met him only a few days ago, but we men from Clare stick together. I'll return the favour when I can. He knows that. Now let's make ourselves comfortable. We'll be here for a while and we'll be last off when we dock." He squeezed her hand gently, not as a lover, not as Tom Lynch had once reached for her in the bracken, but as a friend. She sat down as best she could in the cramped space. In the darkness she allowed herself to cry briefly as the memories of her brother and the boy she adored overwhelmed her and then, as the warmth of the boat crept over her, she fell asleep, curled like a weary toddler with her head on her knees.

The ferry ploughed its way eastward across the wide, silent lake. Even as Kate slept the throb of its engines soothed her fears and, had there been enough light, Peadar would have noticed a smile flicker across her face as a wistful dream took her to Lough Inagh and the valley of her childhood. But later there were other dreams at which she did not smile, of her days on Grosse Isle, of the horrors of the journey on the *Juno*, and further back, of the streets of Galway and the long walk from their village, of Blackstaff and Garrett and their men destroying their houses, and of Tom Lynch, fleeing on the stolen horse and his last defiant cry.

"Boston! Boston!" he had shouted as he galloped across the heather. And now she was on her way to Boston, but determined not to see him again. She was a sinner, a Mary Magdalene, unworthy of someone as good as Tom Lynch. And still she had confessed her guilt to no one.

She woke with a pain churning in her stomach. The ferry had stopped, its engine slowly winding down while the sounds of clanking winch-handles and straining ropes told her they were about to berth.

She felt her belly. It was hard and swollen, her pulse seemed to be racing. She whispered Peadar's name, but his steady breathing told her he was still asleep. She trembled with fear. Something was wrong with the baby, she told herself. Mary had been right. She felt a dizziness rushing at her and her head flopped on to her knees although she no longer felt tired. It was impossible to stand upright in their tiny hiding-place. She knew she must wait. The youth who had smuggled them on board would be back, Peadar had said, but not until the way was clear. She bit her lip and waited.

When the clanking and winching stopped Kate heard the other passengers collecting their possessions, heard them pushing their way along the narrow passageways and their footsteps clattering down the gangway. She listened to the sound of horses' hooves and the grinding of wheels as the coaches headed away to Syracuse with those who had paid their fares.

At last the boat fell silent. Kate shook Peadar's shoulder and as he stirred she heard the bolt being slid back. Suddenly the door was flung open.

"Quick!" said their young friend from Ennis. "They'll be starting the cleaning soon and they'll be looking in here! Follow me!"

They stumbled back along the way they had come, on to the deck and down the gangway. A shout from a man on the ferry's bridge told them they had been seen, but they took no notice of his angry cries and they fled from the quay as fast as they could.

Chapter Thirty

The illness Kate had felt when she woke on the ferry faded as the day wore on. She told herself she had no appetite, that there would be nothing for beggars to eat on the road to Boston and it was as important to keep warm as to eat. She walked on shoulder to shoulder with Peadar while the cold gnawed at her so fiercely it was as if her skin was being torn. It was mid-winter and the land through which they passed lay under snow. By afternoon they had left Syracuse behind them and were headed for Albany. Woods and forests surrounded them on all sides and everywhere there were trees gripped by frost and grasses rigid with cold. A layer of thin cloud hung suspended above their heads, preventing the sun from thawing the land. The rivers and streams they crossed had frozen so hard that not even a drop of water trickled along their courses. No birds braved the air and no animals showed themselves on the ground. Save for a brilliant patch of blood on the snow where a small rodent had been taken by a predator, the road might not have seen a living creature for days.

It seemed to Kate that she and Peadar might be the only beings left alive, indeed she began to doubt that she was alive. But her appetite was proof of her existence, and her hunger, when the nausea allowed, was stronger than ever. She needed to eat, but they both knew they had to keep walking. A couple of times they wheedled a place on a wagon and once a man and his wife in a private carriage took pity on them and stopped and gave them food. But most of the time they trudged on, side by side, unable to speak or unwilling to expend their last reserves of energy on speech. They slept in empty barns, huddled together for warmth, but always the cold woke them and they moved on again.

On the third day, however, they had a stroke of luck. An open cart pulled by a grey cob rattled towards them, driven by a ruddy-faced old man swathed in furs with layers of roughly tanned leather bound round his legs against the cold. Beside him sat a younger man, less protected from the weather but smiling cheerfully all the same. Above the crunch of wheels and the muffled drumming of the horse's hooves on the packed snow the two walkers heard a tune they recognised, a lilting Irish tune. They stopped, bemused, to await the arrival of the vehicle.

It slowed as it drew near and Peadar began to whistle the same tune, his eyes fixed on the smiling passenger whose face lit up even further when he heard the response from the walking figure. The cart stopped and to Kate's astonishment the younger of the two men spoke, just a few words, and in a dialect she did not fully understand, but it was clearly Irish. "Hello," he said. "Have you come far?"

"From Toronto," Peadar replied. "Well, from County Clare really." "And Connemara," Kate added. "We left Toronto three days ago."

"And you're hungry?" asked the young Irishman.

They did not respond but their interrogator needed no answer. He swung his legs over the side of the cart and lowered himself to the ground. "James Galvin," he said, "from Kenmare in County Kerry. If you want I can arrange a bed for you and perhaps a plate of food."

"We've no money," Kate told him, although the thought of food and a bed to appease her hunger and exhaustion almost drove her mad with longing.

The Kerryman stood back theatrically, his hands on his hips as he pretended to study the two travellers. "Is that so?" he said, eyeing their ragged clothes. "And all this while I've been taking you for a couple of millionaires."

He leapt back on to his seat while his silent companion looked on. Then he glanced down at the wretched pair. "Well? We've only got this small load to deliver and then we'll be heading back to Albany. Are you coming or not? We can't wait around all day you know." When they still did not move he laughed and slapped one hand on the driver's arm. "My friend here'll be paying," he said. "He probably doesn't realise it, but he'll be paying."

When Kate's expression still showed disbelief, the young scoundrel merely shook his head at her. "He's as rich as the Queen of England," he smiled, and finally, when Kate still did not move, he added "and he doesn't know a word of Irish either. Come on!" He smiled as if he thought the power of his grin could lift them from the ground.

The house to which the young man took them lay on the outskirts of Albany. At the end of a long, winding driveway bordered by tall, bare-branched chestnut trees, it stood wide and low and pretty, even under the cold mantle of snow which covered its roof and lay in great dunes against its walls. Behind it was a barn, to which their new friend led them, of white-painted wood like the house, and with a pair of rooms to one end, sparsely furnished, but warmed by a log fire smouldering in an iron grate.

"We'll sleep in there," said James Galvin, pointing through a doorway to the smaller of the two rooms in which a couple of straw mattresses and a few blankets could be seen, "and we'll eat here, but not just yet. We're too early."

Kate could see no pots or food and she could hardly ask what it was their new-found friend proposed they should eat, so she took a place near the fire and allowed herself to sink to the floor. She undid the laces of her ill-fitting boots and stretched out her feet to the heat. She unwrapped the shawl from her head and folded it into a pillow. She watched briefly as Peadar followed suit then, although it was early in the afternoon, she lay her head on the shawl and fell straight away to sleep. And no sooner had she begun to sleep than a dream enveloped her, a dream of a new life in a new land, where there would be a house and a bed and a fire and food, even a pair of comfortable shoes. She slept for hours.

The young man, Galvin, slipped out silently, although nothing but an earthquake would have woken the sleeping pair. When he returned late in the afternoon with a bowl of hot stew and a tin can in which sweet chocolate steamed they were still asleep, but he lifted the lid off the dish and he held the chocolate pot under their noses until the glorious smells woke them. Only then did Kate O'Malley believe that her dream might have been true.

They ate as hungry animals might do after a successful hunt, although the food was richer than either of them had ever tasted and the chocolate so sweet that Kate thought, even as she gulped it down, that she might choke on its cloying taste. But there was more than they could eat and the nausea which she had hoped had deserted her returned and she had to sit upright against a wall for a time until it passed.

Later in the night, when the food had settled and James Galvin had put fresh logs on the fire, they talked, wide awake all three of them, as they exchanged stories of their journeys from Ireland.

James spoke of how he had come over from Kerry after the potato crop had failed the first time, in 1845. A winter voyage, he said, colder than he could ever have imagined, and quick, directly to Boston. But there were few jobs in Boston for young Irishmen who could speak no English, and accommodation was almost impossible to find. So he had moved upstate, away from the coast where there were too many immigrants and not enough work.

Anyway he said, he had never wanted to live in a city and Boston was too big for him. He had an older sister there somewhere who had come over with him, but she had fallen for a fellow and didn't want to move away. With the coming of spring he had left her and journeyed up on his own. There was work in the country for a farmer's son like himself, he had his room in the barn, and his master, Mr Hobson, had a housekeeper who thought the world of the young man and cooked whatever he wanted. He sat back with a smile when he had finished and shook the chocolate pot hopefully.

Peadar's story was grimmer, but his natural good humour buoyed him up and he related it with only a slight tremor in his voice. He had come over in 1846, he told them, when the crop had failed a second time. There had been eight of them when they set out for Limerick town, his parents and five sisters as well as himself, but his mother had died before the ship sailed. Their landlord had paid for the passage, but on the cheapest vessel he could find. There was almost no food and not enough water. People began dying almost as soon as they were at sea and three of his sisters had perished before the journey had ended.

His father had disappeared one night as their ship entered the St Lawrence River, his spirit worn away with sadness perhaps, from the strain of losing so many of his family. The captain, unwilling to risk his vessel in the churning waters at the river's mouth, had not turned back.

Peadar had spent his time on Grosse Isle hoping that his father would arrive or that someone would have news of him. But he heard nothing and when his two remaining sisters had died he left the island, determined to get as far away as possible from the land in which his family had perished. He had gone first to Toronto where he had stayed for almost four months. Then, one lucky day, as he put it, he had met Kate, and together they had begun their journey.

James slipped out to refill the chocolate pot when the young man from Clare had finished his story. By the time he returned, Kate was apprehensive. There were too many parts of her story she did not want to relate, too much of which she was ashamed, and too many things she wished she had forgotten. However the young men lay beside her on the floor, their eyes on her face, waiting expectantly. They had told their histories, Peadar said. The fire would last, James added. She must tell her story, they demanded.

So she told of their eviction and the attack on Blackstaff and the policemen, of the walk from Lough Inagh to Galway, of Doctor Browne's charity, of the weeks spent on board the *Juno*, of being turned away from Boston and having to continue their voyage. She told of their arrival on Grosse Isle, of Liam's death, of her release from quarantine, and of meeting up with Peadar in Toronto. She told them of everything except her love for Tom Lynch and the means by which she had obtained food for herself and her brother on their journey. Those things she could not speak of and when she had finished she turned her face away from her audience and stared for a long time into the flames.

They did not dwell that night, none of them, on the meaning of the deaths they had witnessed. It was as if they thought that those who had died had not been chosen to live, and those who had survived had been under the blessing of a God who had selected them as his own, and that his will should not be questioned. They had experienced so much misery that now they were hardened to it. They were alive. They had survived. Nothing else mattered. But, in spite of all they had seen, none of them could understand death.

Yet when Kate allowed, visions of death assailed her from all sides. Bodies in the streets of Galway, bodies being tossed overboard from the *Juno*, the line of small boats removing the dead to the burial-ground on Grosse Isle, and finally, Liam's poor corpse lying in the pit, with nothing but a stone by which he might remember her. Then at last she wept. A feeling of relief crept over her and tears flooded from her eyes in streams until the grime on her cheeks was streaked with a cleanliness as white as the snow banked up on the window ledges outside their warm haven.

She sensed from Peadar's silence that he knew there was more to tell, his eyes never left her face, but he held back his questions and she thanked him silently for that.

Chapter Thirty-One

They stayed in the Hobson barn all the next day
and another night. Much of the time the weary
pair slept and James Galvin, whose winter duties
did not seem too arduous, visited them as often
as he could with bowls of steaming soup and
buttery vegetables, and for dinner half a chicken,
which neither Kate nor Peadar had ever tasted
before. But the rich food was too much for their
wasted stomachs and they slept uneasily, tossing
on their straw beds, disturbed by dreams more
frequently than they would have wished.

On the third day Hobson himself came to see
them, a reserved but friendly man, with news
they were glad to hear. With James translating for
him he spoke to the timid travellers. A coach
was returning east, he said, all the way to Boston,
and it was no more than half full. There were
places for them if they wanted, free places, he
added, as if they thought they might be asked to
pay. The driver was a man he himself employed

from time to time, he told them, and he had agreed to take the young couple with him.

"There," said James Galvin. "You're on your way, though I'll be sorry to see you go. I'll make sure there's food enough for the journey."

They made their farewells the following morning, and the Kerryman, as charming as ever, embraced each of them as dearly as if they had been his own kin. "The best of luck!" he kept repeating. "And if things don't work out you can come back here to see me!" He waved his bright scarf until the coach was out of sight.

The journey started well enough, although there were flurries of snow in the air and the ground had frozen hard during the night. They set off after breakfast and made good time, crossing into Massachusetts in the early afternoon and stopping at nightfall at an inn near the town of Springfield. At the driver's insistence the two young travellers were allowed to sleep above the stable with the warm smell of horse sweat and droppings to remind them of their circumstances. They took out the biscuits they had been given and munched an apple or two, Peadar muttering his appreciation as he swallowed each mouthful.

"This is the life," he said, putting his hands behind his head and lowering himself on to the straw. "I love apples, don't you?"

"Yes. Well, I haven't eaten them often." Kate smiled at him although it was almost too dark to see. For a moment she thought again of Ballyconneely.

"What did you live on, on the boat?" Peadar asked. "Seven or eight weeks was it? What did you have? I mean no boat had that much food on board." He seemed to shake his head in bewilderment. "Or did that fellow you talked about give you food?"

"What fellow?" Kate was indignant. "I talked about no fellow! I was with my brother all the time. I told you, he died on Grosse Isle. There was no one else!"

"I thought there was," Peadar contradicted her. "There was the fellow who attacked the agent, Blackstaff, was it? What did you say that fellow was called?"

"I didn't say." Kate forced the back of her head down on to the straw as if to convince herself she wanted to go to sleep.

"Tom," said Peadar. "You said his name was Tom something."

"Oh, him." Kate's voice showed little interest. "Tom Lynch. He was just someone who lived nearby. Just a neighbour. He wasn't on the boat with us."

"He didn't sound like just a neighbour when you talked about him last night," Peadar said.

"Look. I'm your only friend. If you can't tell me about a fellow, who can you tell? There's nothing you could ask about me that I wouldn't tell. I've no secrets from you. Come on."

"Tom Lynch was a friend of my brother. That's all. I don't even know where he is. He almost killed Blackstaff and then he disappeared." Kate paused, knowing she had made it seem that Tom had run away. "He was right to do it," she added. "He had to go. They'd have hanged him otherwise. He had to go." She sniffed and then to her horror a sob made its way to her throat and blocked her breathing. Peadar's hand came out to her again as it had done on the ferry.

"All right," he whispered. "Now I know enough. He's a lucky fellow, the same Tom Lynch. I hope you find him one day."

"And I hope I never see him again!" Kate hissed fiercely. "So stop talking about him! And if you ever meet up with him you must tell him you never met me in your entire life! D'you hear?"

Peadar was too disappointed to argue. From the emotion in the girl's voice beside him in the darkness he guessed the strength of her feelings for Tom Lynch – and had he been visible to her his unhappiness would have shown.

For her part Kate was more and more troubled. On board the *Juno* she had betrayed everything she believed in. She could never forgive herself for that, although she prayed that it was something she would put behind her some day. She had disgraced herself and her family, even if so far she had managed to hide her pregnancy. Except for Peadar and Mary, both of whom had guessed, nobody knew of her condition, but then in America, she told herself, nobody knew her anyway, so it hardly mattered.

In Montreal, when she first realised she was pregnant, she had not allowed herself to dwell on the matter. She calculated that if the baby was born at all it would arrive in March and by then she would be long gone from Canada, settled in some softer clime to the south. Secretly she believed that the child would not survive, that her own hunger would deny the baby any chance of life and that soon, somewhere on the road perhaps, or in some dark corner, she would lose the child, and the problem it posed would melt away.

Of her pregnancy she was not in doubt, nor of the identity of the father. For that reason too she hoped to lose the child, for on every occasion when she thought of it, Axel's face reared up at her, so close and real she could almost smell him, and if the child did not come into existence, Kate told herself, she would not have to think of its father.

She would not talk of her condition to Peadar, although she knew he had not failed to notice it. Her pregnancy became a secret they shared but never acknowledged. In her innocent mind it would always be a stain, her secret, and she could never forgive herself for it, but it was *her* secret. It was the secret which Tom Lynch must never discover. That was the reason she would not stay long in Boston.

Chapter Thirty-Two

The long separation from Kate O'Malley had
hardened Tom Lynch to his plight. He missed her
as much as if she was one of his own limbs and it
had become so painful to think of her and
imagine her whereabouts or her progress towards
him that he, like Kate herself, had vowed to put
his love from his mind. If he could not be with
her, he told himself, he would not torment
himself by dreaming of her. He would find her
one day, he knew, and soon, he hoped, but for
the present he forced himself to accept his
loneliness.

The discovery that Garrett was in New York
quite broke the young man's resolve. Back
flooded the memories of Lough Inagh, of
Ballyconeelly, of Kate's upturned face and her
sweet mouth. He ached with longing to see her
and hold her. His stay in New York had been
tolerated only as a preparation for going to
Boston to meet her, but Garrett's appearance

outside the shebeen had changed everything. He knew he had to flee as soon as possible.

When Tom Lynch decided he must leave New York his first thought was to head west, away from the cities of the east coast in which most of his compatriots had settled. But he said nothing of his plans and he told no one the cause of his departure. He knew he could confide in nobody.

Pointedly he asked one of his friends the cheapest way to travel to Philadelphia. He left his job, telling his employer he was thinking of crossing the continent to California. He told his workmates not to expect to see him again in New York. He spoke loudly of going south or west. He purchased a ticket on a coach to Baltimore, asking the man who sold it how soon he could continue on to Georgia or the Carolinas. He enquired about prospects for work in New Orleans. He spread as many false trails as he could and less than two days after his encounter with Garrett, he rose at dawn, rolled his possessions into a meagre bundle and walked to the southernmost tip of Manhattan Island. There, observed by no one who knew him, he boarded a boat.

Chapter Thirty-Three

The day on which Kate O'Malley and Peadar FitzGibbon came to Boston was as bleak as any the pair had seen on their journey. The air was stiff with cold, and flurries of sleet were spat at them from clouds which hovered like vultures above their heads. The towering city of stone which Kate had seen from the deck of the *Juno* five months earlier could not be recognised as they approached the ramshackle outskirts of the town, and Kate found herself wanting to turn back, wondering why she had allowed herself to be persuaded to come to Boston at all.

It was Peadar who had brought her this far, she complained to herself, Peadar who had persuaded her to come, poor innocent Peadar who had no idea that there might be someone in Boston she must not see, or who must not see her. She wished with all her might that she had gone directly to Baltimore, far to the south, where no one would recognise her or question

231

her or even show surprise at her condition. In Baltimore she could have been no one. In Baltimore her life would have been her own, her past would have been behind her.

But fear and weariness had worn her down and she had no reserves of energy. She knew she had to rest, that her body was exhausted, and although she dreaded entering the city which for so long had been her destination she offered no resistance as Peadar took her arm and led her into the crowded streets.

To Kate O'Malley and Peadar FitzGibbon, Boston was overwhelming, several times larger than Toronto and, if possible, less human. There had been a swaggering confidence about the Canadian town which the older city had outgrown. Boston was a place of sobriety and formality. The streets were swept clean each morning, at night they were lit, carriages clanked in orderly lines along the wide avenues while the gentlemen and ladies of the city greeted each other with a restraint bordering on coldness.

In 1848 there was already an underclass in Boston, a ghetto of people whose dark skin so surprised Kate when first she saw them that she almost fainted with alarm. These were the blacks, emancipated slaves from the southern states mainly, or escapees still in fear of discovery and recapture by their masters. To this impoverished group had fallen the most menial tasks the city had to offer. They were tolerated, these unfortunates, but their lives were harsh. They lived apart in the rough tenements of the city's North End and they were prepared to fight to protect their already difficult position in the hierarchy of Boston. They did not welcome the arrival of the Irish.

Indeed, in Boston there was little welcome for the poor at any time. The old Yankee city exercised its charitable instincts by sending money and food back across the Atlantic. It did not want the poor of Europe arriving destitute in its streets, and in 1848, when the town had long since closed its port to ships arriving from the pestilent, famine-struck island across the northern ocean, those Irish who managed to reach the city were treated with an abhorrence which even the English would have considered extreme.

There was no work in Boston for those without clothes to wear and no habitable accommodation for those who could not keep themselves clean and whose hair was matted with weeks or months of salt and grime. There were few opportunities for those who could speak no word of English to learn it, and no food for those unable to earn enough to buy it. For the vast majority of the Irish, Boston was a desert set in a tantalising oasis.

The destitute new immigrants were rejected by every other group in the city and they reacted accordingly. They had no option but to throng the streets as they had done in the cities of Canada; no option but to beg or steal, to attack the residents for their clothes or their purses; no option but to kill if it was necessary to remain alive.

The city created another class of them, as little respected as the stray dogs and cats which roamed the streets. The rich ignored them, the middle classes treated them with contempt and the workers, white and black alike, protested their presence at every opportunity. The Irish became a class of their own, the lowest of the low; their violence grew and soon they were feared as much as they were loathed.

They roamed the streets in gangs hundreds strong, terrifying those on whom they preyed, outwitting and outnumbering the authorities and making normal life almost impossible for the residents of the city, that haven of wealth and peace and decorum.

Soon even the poorest areas of the town became uninhabitable to their former residents. Those who could sold their houses and moved out, away from the robbers and thugs who daily threatened them. Those who could not sell, or who would not sell at the low prices which the arrival of the immigrants had brought about, converted their once proud mansions into tenements. And in poured the Irish. Hundreds, thousands of them, four to a room, eight to a room, twenty to a room, in rooms which had once held little more than a single bed or a piano. More than a hundred people to a house in which one well-to-do family might have lived with a few servants.

There were almost no facilities for cooking or washing, even if the wretches had had food or clothes, and there was no such thing as furniture. Often the floors could not take the weight of numbers and whole buildings collapsed. Ventilation was inadequate and in the heat of summer the new occupants broke open the windows and doors to allow the breeze to freshen the air. By winter the cold was intolerable. There was no water. The drains were unable to service the numbers using them. Everyone was ill. Fevers broke out, fevers no doctor had seen before. Typhus spread throughout the city, controlled only by the fires which sprang up from time to time, destroying whole blocks in a night and leaving homeless again a thousand or more wretched inhabitants.

It was into one of these tenement hell-holes that Peadar took Kate. By the middle of January her condition showed clearly and her skin had once again taken on the pallid, sickly look she had lost temporarily on Grosse Isle. She was feeble, and quite incapable of looking for work even if there had been work for her.

The tiny room they occupied was little more than a cupboard on the top floor of an old house in a street of many others and once Kate had climbed the stairs the first time she knew she would hardly be able to do so again. They had no regular means of paying rent, but Peadar was clever and he had become a skilful thief. With the proceeds of his crimes he could feed them, and from time to time make some contribution to the landlord.

Life on the streets did not suit Peadar. He had no choice but to steal, but he was not at ease with himself. He suggested once or twice that they leave Boston. He reminded Kate of what James Galvin had said as the three of them lay before his fire.

"Couldn't I get work there, Kate?" he asked, "and you too, once you're able for it?"

"Perhaps," Kate replied, "but not yet. I couldn't travel now, Peadar. Later maybe, in the spring." Her voice weakened and she feared she might cry as the thought of a warm fire disturbed her unhappiness.

Even Peadar's spirits were lowered by the persistent gloom. He became careless and once he was so nearly caught while lifting the purse of a merchant's stout wife that he swore to give up his life of crime.

For a few days he trudged the streets, walking as tall as he could and forcing a sparkle to his eye even when no joy survived. He pushed himself to the front of every queue, knocked on every door, plied every foreman with eager questions, pursued every tradesman's wagon he could see, but to no avail. There was no work for him. After a week of honesty he had no choice but to return to the street corner where he knew he could make a living. He wore his dejection like a shroud.

For her part Kate too had lost all hope. She had calculated the date of her child's arrival. The earliest it could be born was in March, eight or so weeks away, and she feared that her spirit would not last that long even if her body could carry on. For much of each day she slept, tended on occasion by one or other of the women who shared the room closest to hers. But there was nothing to do except wait.

To pass the time and in order to keep Kate's spirits from sinking Peadar would relate fanciful stories to her, wildly exaggerated anecdotes of his life in County Clare. He would stretch out beside her on the floor and rest his head on one hand. "'Twas such a day," he would begin. He would settle down next to the makeshift bed on which Kate lay and he would smile at her as if they had not a care in the world. "The whole village would be there, and the sun would be splitting the stones in the fields. The streets would be filled with young girls dancing and young men tapping their toes to the music. There'd be food everywhere, tables and tables of it, bread and potatoes and meat and . . . and . . . " but here he would run out of words, having known no food other than potatoes, and he would go on to describe the music or the dancing or the golden evening light which would flood the blue sky of Clare as the sun slipped below Slieve Callan.

Then he might close his eyes, to block his tears, Kate sometimes thought, but he would smile blindly and carry on speaking. "And after we'd eaten our fill the girls would come over to us and ask us to dance and I, being one of the best dancers around, would be brushing them off until someone special came up to me. Then everyone else would stop and there's be just the two of us, twirling and turning and flinging ourselves about until the fiddler would howl for mercy and put down his bow to stop his arm from falling off with exhaustion!"

By this time Kate would be smiling and shaking her head to show her admirer she no longer believed him, but Peadar would be unabashed.

"And she'd be looking into my eyes as we danced, wanting to be kissed, by me of course, and then what d'you think I'd do, Kate?"

Kate would raise one doubting eyebrow to return the question.

"I'd kiss her of course," the young man would boast, "while even her father and brothers were watching!"

"What was this one's name, Peadar?" Kate would tease him. "Was it Maura, or Síle or Gránia this time?" And she would smooth one hand across her hair to remind him that she too was a woman.

Suddenly Peadar's confidence would ebb and he would stop his wild gesticulating and let his hands fall to his sides.

"Oh, I can't remember," he would say. "She wasn't anything to me. Just a dancing partner, you know. She meant nothing."

So Kate in turn would have to make up a tale, but she was less inventive than the young man and her stories were constrained by the sight of her swollen belly and the loneliness of her life, and all her memories revolved around Tom Lynch of whom she could not speak. She needed to have the baby, she told herself, and to forget Tom. She needed to start a new life. Once the birth was over, she believed, everything would be different, although she had no idea what she might do or how she would care for the infant. She did not want to join the rabble on the streets again. Not that she despised them; Peadar was one of them after all, and it was only because he was part of that rabble that he was able to keep her alive. But she saw herself as something else. She imagined her parents watching her, wondering what she was doing, wondering even if she was alive. Her family seemed so distant now – her memories of them so faint. Whenever she imagined them it was against the background of Lough Inagh that they appeared, although she knew there was little likelihood of their being there. They would be in the poorhouse in Galway, she supposed, if they were still alive that was, and even to be alive might be a miracle. Apart from the note Liam had asked Axel to take back with him she had made no attempt to contact her parents, had done nothing to inform them of Liam's death. She did not know how to write, and if ever she thought of them it was always with guilt that they occupied her mind so rarely.

At times she would conjure up a picture of her mother, willing her careworn face to appear, at times even speaking to the vision in her mind's eye, asking what her mother would do if she were present and able to help. No answer came of course. How could her mother even begin to imagine life in Boston, her daughter alone all day in a tiny room, in a wretched house, with a stranger's child in her belly and a thief below in the street, stealing to feed her?

By now winter had settled on Boston and the broken windows of the room in which Kate lay could do nothing to keep out the cold. Gusts of snow and sleet drifted in to lie around her on the floor, so bright and sparkling that they might have looked beautiful in another setting, but here they lay for hours, chilling the room and dampening the air until one of the neighbouring women brushed them away, leaving the floor wet and stained.

Kate's spirits sank lower each day and by the end of January, if she had had the strength and had known how, she would even have taken her own life. She thought constantly of how she could turn her back on Peadar, but how could she leave him after all he was doing for her? She knew he loved her, he had told her so many times, but she could not imagine anyone wanting to overlook her condition and her helplessness. She could see herself only as a burden, and the more time she had to reflect on her situation the more she hoped she might die.

Peadar tried his best to kindle her enthusiasm for life but to little avail. Kate responded to his smiles and his attempts at conversation with a wry grin which failed to disguise her despair. She pushed from her mind any thoughts of her family or the past. She forced herself, whenever Tom's face appeared before her, to think of something else, to forget their friendship, to tell herself that she had never been to Ballyconneely and walked on the sand and stolen fruit and laughed with her brother and his friend as they wandered the roads of Connemara. When one dark afternoon she recalled again the night they had slept in the bracken, she found herself physically pushing from her the memory of his warm hand reaching for hers, of the fruit he had given her and the way he had lain his cheek on her palm. She wept for hours after that, but she had succeeded. She did not think of Tom Lynch again.

For Peadar the burden of caring for the young girl was one he could easily bear. It was only a matter of months since his own sisters had died, the last two of them in his arms, just as Liam had died in Kate's, and he ached with loneliness and the need for someone to whom he could devote himself. From the first day he had met Kate he had fallen for her and now, even knowing that she carried the child of another man beneath her swollen skirts (Tom Lynch's child, he assumed, knowing nothing of the Dutchman and the events on board the *Juno*), he would have married her instantly had she accepted him.

242

But although Kate's smile was warm and her friendship genuine, she did not love Peadar. Her smile was the smile of a sister for a brother and her friendship was distant, as if she could see a barrier between them which he could not.

He was undeterred, however. He was determined to support her whatever his chances of winning her, and the more he could do for her, he thought, the better his chances would be. He brought her food as often as he could, he sat with her during the long cold nights when she could not sleep, he gave up his only blanket in order that she might be warm and when her hand trembled with fear or her lip quivered at the thought of what lay before her he would touch her forehead gently or stroke her cheek with a fingertip. She came to trust him completely, she looked forward to the times he spent with her, she wept when he told her he loved her, but she did not love him in return.

All the time the pains in her stomach grew worse. She could feel the baby moving inside her and her fear and dread alarmed her more and more. She had no one to turn to, no one to whom she could explain her circumstances. She did not even bother trying to explain to the other women in the house that Peadar was neither her husband nor the father of the child she was carrying.

Her body was wasting away. Her hair had grown lank and drab and her skin was, if anything, greyer and more waxen than it had been on board the *Juno* during those fearful days she wanted to forget. The boots Peadar had stolen for her in Toronto had completely worn out on the journey to Boston and her clothes were hardly recognisable as such. She had no means of washing them and no others to wear while they were being washed. She lay almost naked under her stolen blanket, shivering as much from despair as from the frightful cold which had struck the city. She could easily have died and at times she prayed that death would come to her. That, she thought, might be the only solution to her problems.

Peadar, meanwhile, found the strength to renew his optimism. Between the hours he spent each day on the streets stealing or begging he continued to search for work and one evening when it seemed that all doors were closed to him, luck fell his way. He had spoken to a young man sweeping the streets, well, not the streets, he explained to Kate, but the sidewalks outside some of the better shops in the city. He was a friendly young fellow, Peadar said, from Mayo or Galway if his accent was anything to go by, and he seemed to know everyone in Boston. He even said there was work to be had for those who looked hard enough for it.

He had taken Peadar to see the manager of one of the shops and the following morning Peadar was employed. Only for as long as the snow lasted, the manager warned, but at eight cents an hour and the warmth of the workroom for a few minutes a day. Even Kate's spirits were lifted to see the joy in her friend's face when he told her the news and she praised him with a smile which only encouraged his love. By stealing at night and sweeping snow by day, Peadar was able to return to their room each evening with food for both of them and, by the end of the first week, with almost three dollars in his pocket.

"Who is he, this new friend?" Kate asked as she picked crumbs of sweet cake from her blanket.

"Éamonn, he told me his name was. He said he'd been here a while but he doesn't talk much about himself. I want him to meet you. Maybe I'll bring him here one day."

"Look at me, Peadar." Kate's hands signalled her shame. "You can't bring anyone here! I don't want visitors. You didn't tell him anything about me did you?"

"Just that you exist and that I love you. Nothing else."

"Not my name or that I'm . . . this way?" She let her fingers fall on to the mound of her stomach and thrust out her jaw demanding the truth.

"Nothing. Not your name and nothing at all about the . . . the . . . baby."

"Don't say the word, Peadar. Don't say the word, 'baby'. I know it's there. I know I've a baby inside me, but what am I to do with no wedding ring and no father? It's not to be talked about, Peadar. Not by anyone. I don't want to be discussed by you or Éamonn or anybody else. Do you understand?"

The young man from Clare did not answer for a while. He stood with his hands clenched, wanting to speak but afraid of the effect his words might have. But eventually he found the words, or perhaps he found the strength to say the words which he knew had to be spoken.

"You're going to have this baby, Kate. You can do nothing about it now, so why hide it? Everyone here knows. You're tired all the time, you've a huge bulge under your skirt, you can hardly climb the stairs. What are you going to do when it arrives? You can't pretend then, not when it's screaming and bawling and you're having to feed it and change it. You'll have to stop pretending then."

In his determination he spoke with his eyes closed, opening them only after a long silence told him something was wrong, that he had gone too far and offended her.

When he looked at Kate again she had turned to the wall, unnaturally still, and when he bent to reassure her she tossed her shoulder at him angrily, shaking him off, refusing to allow him to touch even her hand.

But he would not leave her unconvinced. "You have to stop pretending, Kate," he repeated. "There's not long to go now," he paused, "and I'll marry you today if only you'll have me."

She turned away from him in silence and he could do nothing but shake his head disconsolately at her back.

Chapter Thirty-Four

Two days later the pains had become so bad that Kate could no longer sit upright. She lay, surrounded by small drifts of snow which even the regular attentions of her neighbours could not keep from building up around her, her scrawny body on one side and her knees pulled up to her waist to lessen the agonies caused by the living thing growing and kicking within her. Spasms wracked her abdomen and hips, forcing her at night, when her neighbours were sleeping, to gnaw on the knuckles of her hands to stop herself from crying out and waking the other occupants of the building.

Then one morning when she least expected it, the pains eased and she stretched out on the floor, allowing herself to relax. There were still several weeks to go before the baby was due, but she could tell from its movements that it was not going to be denied. She had woken to find on her legs a mixture of blood and something else, something she did not recognise, but which she knew had come from that part of her where the child waited.

It came quickly. The pains were no worse than she had feared and the labour was brief. An hour, perhaps a little more, and then with a haste which surprised her the tiny child arrived, a boy, screaming and coughing and dribbling, his puckered rosebud mouth sucking the air as eagerly as any calf or lamb and his fingers clutching at nothing, as if to feed on that too if no food was put his way.

She took him to her breast as Peadar watched, and together they cried as the infant took life and sucked at the shrunken teat she offered it.

It was a weak baby. Even the least knowledgeable of parents could see that it would take a miracle for it to survive in the inhospitable surroundings of its home, but there was a determination in its eyes and movements which surprised them both. The child spent every waking hour searching for food and would not sleep without satisfying itself that it had done its best for that day.

In spite of her fears Kate wasted no time in deciding she loved the child more than she had loved anything else in her short life and she named him Patrick in honour of her father. She found the energy to bring the baby each day to a place where she could wash it, she wrapped it in cloth as soft as Peadar could find, she warmed it with the heat from her own body and she fed it as best she could with the milk she produced herself.

In spite of the appalling conditions – to which it was oblivious – the baby thrived. Its skin filled, its stomach swelled and its limbs waved with an energy which seemed to have no source. Tuffs of hair sprouted from its bald scalp and nails hardened at the tips of its fingers and toes. It grimaced when the pangs of hunger struck, and when it was sated by the milk of its mother it fell back with a grin as contented as that of an old man sucking at a glass of ale.

But the months of hunger had taken their toll on Kate's health and as her son grew stronger her own body weakened. Her eyes sank deep into their sockets and the flesh of her fingers and arms, which was all that an onlooker could see of her, shrivelled on her bones. Her shoulders drooped and her breasts flattened and dried as the child drained her. Only one of them could be the winner in this battle for life, Peadar knew, and Kate too was not unaware that the child would destroy her if she allowed it.

The disinterest she had felt in her own life in the days before the birth returned again. She saw the child as a reincarnation of herself, continuing the life she had begun but was unworthy to continue. She convinced herself that it was unimportant which of them survived, that her own life was worthless to anyone else and that the baby would make a better candidate for the human race than herself. She devoted herself to ensuring only that the child lived.

Nature, however, which pays no heed to the wishes of the poor humans whose destinies it controls, had other ideas. Nature saw on the one hand a child with no future without a mother, and on the other a mother who had a chance of survival so long as she did not have to feed a child. As if on cue the baby began to weaken. One late afternoon when its cries became too much for Kate to bear in her cramped room and there was no coaxing it to take food, from either its mother's breast or a warm thumb, she got up from her bed and wrapped herself in whatever rags she could find.

It was early evening and Peadar was still at his work when she left. She took up the child and, barefoot, walked slowly down the stairs which had imprisoned her for so long, on to the streets where her countrymen and women swarmed in thieving gangs. She had heard talk of a hospital somewhere close by and she found her way there, although it took her more than an hour. She had no knowledge of such places and when she arrived, finding no one who could understand her Irish, she simply thrust the baby into the arms of the first nurse she saw.

But the immigrants were not welcome at the hospital. The nurse screamed at the imposition thrust upon her by the filthy young woman in rags. "Take it away!" she cried in English. "This place is not for you! Go away! Go away!"

Kate took back the silent bundle which was her child and looked about her in desperation. "He's dying," she pleaded, trying to catch the attention of one of the faces averted from her. "He'll die tonight."

The people around her had the excuse of being unable to understand her. They felt no need to help. For a while she waited, imploring the onlookers with her glances, but no one responded to her pleas. Eventually she walked from the hospital with the child in her arms and lifting her nose to the air she followed the smell of salt and fish and tar which she knew would lead her to the harbour.

The baby cried incessantly as she walked, and from time to time she stopped to soothe it, kissing its cheek or its forehead or its eyes and whispering to it in a voice so soft that no passer-by could hear her. "I love you, Patrick," she said. "I am with you. It is too cold here, you need not stay. I will hold you, child. I will hold you as you go."

In time she found her way on to the wharves where there were few lights and broad patches of darkness. She flitted about like a moth, one minute wishing to be invisible and the next wanting to be seen, or perhaps needing to see the weakening child in her arms. There was no pattern to her movements, no reason for turning either to left or to right. She meandered like a grazing deer or a youngster at play in a wide open field. The fear and the anguish and the humiliation had all left her, She was free now, all control gone, her attention given over to the face of the infant dying in her arms, so absorbed in the child that she was unaware of herself, unaware even of the slow icy wind which flung dust in her eyes and grappled with her shawl and withered the hair on her head.

Finally she stood at the end of one of the wharves against which a ship could lie to take on or give up its cargo. The pier was vacant. A Swedish trader lay at anchor thirty or forty yards off, its hull washed by a dark sea so heavy with cold that hardly a ripple broke its surface. For almost an hour she stood quite still. She could see no movement on the ship's deck. She felt herself completely alone. The baby cried from time to time and from its perfect mouth came the sounds of sucking which no mother could refuse. But Kate was dry of milk. There was no reason, she thought, to torment her son with an empty teat and after a while his crying stopped. She could hear him breathing still, and feel his warmth, but she knew it would not be for much longer. A few minutes later she moved to the edge of the wharf, crossed herself and closed her eyes.

As she let his body go she knew he was dead. For a time she had thought of jumping with him, of burying his pale, pinched face in the soft flesh of her breast and holding him until together they could see the welcome of God's smile. But something held her back, some urge to live gave her strength and she let him fall alone. As she heard the splash the wind seemed to strengthen, sleet whitened the air and waves began to ruffle the harbour's surface. Her child was gone. She turned and walked away. The streets were not deserted but through the slums of Boston no one noticed her. Save for her tears she was indistinguishable from a thousand others like her on the pavements that night.

Somehow she found the tenement building in which she and Peadar lived. She climbed the stairs and entered their room. She unwrapped the damp shawl from her shoulders and lay down, shaking with cold. She prayed that she would sleep and not wake. She prayed that she would not have to face another day.

Chapter Thirty-Five

When Peadar returned he found her lying on her back like a corpse, her eyes half shut and the skin of her face falling back on to her cheekbones as if her skull had forced its way unnaturally forward. Except for the warmth of her breath on his hand he might have assumed she had already left him.

He wasted no time. He turned and ran down the stairs and out of the building as fast as he could. He ran to where the young man called Éamonn lived. Éamonn who had got him work, who knew everything about Boston, who knew a doctor. An Irish doctor what was more, who could come to Kate, who could save her, who could bring warmth to her body and comfort to her bones and a smile to her sweet face.

In a building not far away he found the young man he sought, lying with five or six others on the floor of an unfurnished room. Playing cards lay scattered on the floor beside a half empty whiskey bottle. A blanket had been hung across the open window to keep out the cold. The room was full of smoke and laughter and good humour. Children had gathered at the doorway. A dog lay snoring at the feet of one of the gamblers. Éamonn looked up, guarded but welcoming, his brown eyes wide open to question the unexpected visitor. With his free hand he brushed the black curling hair from his forehead.

"It's her," Peadar said. "The girl I told you about. The one I live with. Something's happened, I don't know what it is. She went out. She was caught in the sleet. She's so cold. I think she's dying." He looked around the room. The game had stopped. All eyes were upon him and he could no longer speak.

"What can I do?" Éamonn put down his cards, and began to stand. "Well? Tell me. What do you want me to do?"

"You said you knew a doctor. She must have a doctor. She's dying. She needs help."

"He won't come out at this hour." Éamonn shook his head as if to confirm his statement. "Not to a tenement."

"She'll not last the night. Please come with me." Peadar held out his hands, imploring his friend to help.

Éamonn flung down his cards and stepped across the circle of men with whom he had been playing. Peadar grasped him by the arm and dragged him down the stairs and out into the street.

Éamonn tried to talk as they made their way to the room where Kate lay. "So who is she, this girl you love so much but who doesn't love you?" If the face of his companion had not shown such fear he would have continued in his casual manner, but Peadar's brows were low and his mouth was set in a grim line. They marched on.

"Where did you say she was from?" Éamonn asked to break the silence.

In his anxiety, Peadar forgot his vow not to speak of Kate's history. "Connemara," he answered. "Somewhere called Lough Inagh."

"Lough Inagh?" Éamonn turned, grabbing his companion by both shoulders. "Lough Inagh!" he shouted. "I . . . I . . . I've been there! I know Lough Inagh! Who is she? What is her name?" He was almost crying, in a frenzy of which Peadar had never thought him capable. "Who is she?"

"It's for her to tell you her name if she wants. I swore I'd tell no one."

Éamonn stared at him in panic. "Where is she? Take me there, man! Take me there!"

Together they ran along darkened streets, past groups of beggars, and thieves lurking in the shadows. They rounded a corner and sped across the slippery snow to the doorway of the tenement, up the stairs and into the room where Peadar had left Kate only a few minutes before.

She had not moved. She lay perfectly still. A woman sat beside her, a mug of broth in her hands which she was holding to the girl's lips. Another blanket had been placed over Kate's body but even with the added weight Peadar could see that the shivering had not stopped.

The instant he caught sight of her, the visitor fell to his knees, placing a hand at either side of her face as Peadar looked on, astonished at their sudden intimacy.

"Is it you, Kate?" the young stranger whispered, as tears filled his eyes. It was not a question but a greeting. "It's me, Tom. Tom Lynch. I am here, Kate. Where have you been for so long?"

Kate's eyes flickered briefly at the sound of the newcomer's voice. For a moment it seemed she was trying to speak but no words came from her.

"You must live for me, Kate!" the young man cried. "I've waited so long for this! You must live!"

"She might live," said the woman with the broth, "but she'll have a better chance if you let me get some of this into her. The poor lass, and the wee mite gone too. What a thing to happen." She slid her hand under the neck of the motionless girl and lifted up her head. A few drops of the hot liquid trickled down Kate's throat, but she made no effort to swallow them. The woman lowered her head again.

For a while longer Kate lay as if dead, then without warning her eyes fell open and she caught sight of the face above her own. "Who is it?" she murmured. "Is that you, Tom?"

Her visitor nodded. She spoke again. "I said I'd meet you in Boston, didn't I?" She smiled her recognition at him, a smile Peadar had not seen before, a smile he had hoped would one day be directed at himself.

Then Éamonn, or was it Tom, Peadar had no idea now of the name of his friend, placed a hand under Kate's head and gently turned her until one cheek rested on his palm as his had once lain on hers so long ago in the days when they had been happy together.

Slowly, almost imperceptibly, a smile of contentment stole over the pale face of the girl and Tom Lynch brushed her forehead with his lips.

Kate turned to Peadar. There was no joy in his face. "My dearest friend," she said, "who did so much for me. I can never thank you enough."

Peadar knew then that he had lost her, but he felt no anger towards his rival. He had never before seen love kindled by a smile, nor life restored by a touch. The weariness which had dragged Kate down for so long seemed to have been banished as her thin arms enfolded the body of the young man kneeling over her.

A silence enveloped them and then the warmth of their love seemed to flood into the room, driving out the cold and misery and squalor as Kate whispered his name over and over again as if it had become a prayer. "Tom," she murmured, "Tom, Tom, Tom," and she smiled again as she kissed away the tears which streamed from her lover's eyes.

Boston
June 18th 1855

Dearest Mammy,

My hand is shaking so much I can hardly write. I still can't believe I saw your name on the list in church this morning. It's more than seven years since I gave your name to Father Murray and since then I've heard nothing. Father Murray is our priest and he spends most of his days trying to find the families of us who came over during the hunger.

When we heard how bad it had got in Ireland, after Liam and me got away, I didn't think you would still be alive, but Tom made me put your name down. This morning I was in church. I'd stopped looking at the lists long ago. I'd looked so many times before. I used to read them every day in the hope I'd see your names, but after a while I couldn't bring myself to read them. It used to hurt so much when I'd look and there'd be nothing there for me.

But this morning I read the list and there you were, Mary O'Malley from Lough Inagh, mother of Kate and Liam. I think I fainted Mammy. All I know is one minute I was looking at the list and then I was lying on a seat at the back of the church and someone was sprinkling water on my face.

Anyway, back I came and called in to see Tom on the way. He was in the shop but he closed it for the day and came home with me to help me with the letter.

Yes it's me who is writing it, Mammy. We both speak English now and we've learnt to read and write it as well. I can't spell Irish at all so I have to write in English and hope you'll find someone who'll read it to you.

Will you write to me as soon as you can? I don't know how to ask this, but the list didn't tell anything but your name and I don't know if Da is still alive or Jack and Mae and Danny and Áine.

Liam is dead Mammy. I can't say it any other way. He died with me in Canada, on Grosse Isle where we had to stop for the quarantine. It was terrible on the ship and he got the fever. I loved him Mammy. I did my best to look after him, but I couldn't keep him alive. I'd have died for him you know and there were times I wished I had.

I don't know what you are doing now or who's still with you. Do you want to come to America, Mammy? If you do we'll help you. We have money for the fare, for all of you if you want. There are houses here and work for everybody.

Tom and I are married seven years now. We have four children and we have a shop. First we had three girls, Mary and Rose and Gránia, and I've a boy just a year old. I called him Liam, Mammy, and I'd die for him too.

We have a house of our own. It's not big like some of the houses in Boston, but it's what we dreamed of when the times were bad. We've two fireplaces, Mammy, with a chimney for each. There's a parlour and a kitchen with a table and seven chairs and a bedroom for Tom and me and two more rooms for the children and all the rooms have real glass windows so we're warm in winter and cool in summer, just like real Americans.

The house is made of wood but we painted it white and I have a garden with flowers, and apples and plums that Tom planted for me, and a sycamore tree. I grow cabbages too and all sorts of things you never saw in your life, like carrots and turnips and pumpkins. I don't grow potatoes though, Mammy. I never want to grow them. If we want potatoes we buy them.

Oh, Mammy I want to see you so bad it hurts. Please send word that you'll come over to us. Now I know you're alive I'll not rest until I can see you. I think you'd be proud of me, Mammy.

Tom and I send all our love.
Your loving daughter,
Kate Lynch.